THE SPORTING PARLOR

THE SPORTING PARLOR

WANDA LANE

CUTTING EDGE

Previously released as "The Red House on Green Street"

ISBN-13: 978-1-970848-06-9

Published by
Cutting Edge Books
PO Box 8212
Calabasas, CA 91372
www.cuttingedgebooks.com

CHAPTER ONE

I was in the kitchen when John came home at noon. I sensed what he was going to say and what was going through his mind. He set his lunch pail on the table as if he was through with it forever. He stood there, staring at me, his hands shoved deep into his pockets.

"I can't make anything on that lousy job," he said.

I didn't say anything. I stood beside the sink and looked at him. John looked funny in overalls and work shirt, almost like a different person.

"Hell, Honey, there's no sense in my slaving for peanuts when you're sitting on a gold mine," he continued. "How would you like to go back to earning some real money?"

I tried to think of something to say, but it had all been said before. I didn't want to be a prostitute again, yet I knew that it was useless to argue. I had said yes once and I knew I would say it again this time. I didn't feel like going through the arguments and fights again. John lit a cigarette, came over to where I stood and put his arm around my waist.

"Hell, it's just a job," he said softly. He held the cigarette to my lips. "You know I'll always love you, Baby."

He had a way of talking and looking at me that turned my insides to water. He could make me believe that white was black and black was white and saying yes when I should be saying no. I knew that I should have been telling him that prostitution was indecent, immoral, wicked and wrong, and that no decent woman would ever think of stooping so low. But when you love a guy, it makes things different.

"What kind of a joint is it?" I asked. John shrugged his shoulders.

"Just another whorehouse, that's all I can tell you," he broke into a smile and patted my behind. "Do you want me to take ten bucks and investigate?"

"You do and I'll break your neck!" I answered, feeling anger rise inside me.

I knew he was teasing, but I couldn't take that kind of teasing. I think I would have killed him if I ever found him with another woman. John just laughed and hugged me. I could feel the excitement beating in his body.

"The Madame is coming this afternoon to look over the factory," he said casually. "You can ask her all about it."

I shot him a startled look. I didn't want anyone seeing me looking like this, faded jeans, one of John's old white shirts with the tail out, and run-over slippers.

"Why didn't you have her wait until tomorrow?" I complained, "My hair—it's a mess."

"You've got a couple of hours," John set the coffee pot on the stove. "She won't be here until three."

I pretended that I wasn't eager when I walked towards our bedroom, but I was. I had known that sooner or later, John would put me back on the turf. I had been dreading it, but now that he had done it, I was almost glad. I was bored with housework and keeping up our apartment and there had been times when I secretly wished I was back at Blanche's.

"You said something about ten bucks. Is that what the girls are getting?" I stopped at the door and turned to look at John.

"That's what I heard."

"Yeah, but what do I have to do for ten bucks?"

"The same thing you did at Blanche's for five."

I didn't know whether to believe John or not. I took a bath and used his razor to shave under my arms. I needed a permanent and wished John had given me warning so I could have got one before the Madame saw me. Suddenly, I had to laugh. Six months ago, I had been afraid the Madame *would* accept me, now I was afraid she wouldn't. Three months in a brothel had done that to me.

I carefully picked over my lingerie to find a bra and some panties that I thought would be suitable. Then I couldn't decide what else to wear, a dress, a robe, or a pair of pajamas. I asked John and he suggested that I wear just a housecoat. I picked out some beads and earrings that I thought would become me and when I put them on, my hands were shaking with excitement.

I stopped, lit a cigarette and studied my face in the mirror. I *wanted* to be a prostitute again. I *wanted* to hear men ask for me and listen to their footsteps coming down the hall to my room. This desired showed in my face and eyes. I had looked upon my three months at Blanche's as being a living hell at the time, but now I wanted to go back to it. I didn't have time to figure it out because John called to tell me that we had company. I blotted my lipstick and went into the living room.

Our guest was seated on the sofa and John was beside her. She was about forty-five, perhaps fifty, a tall thin woman, almost bony, with dyed red hair. On her left arm were a number of bracelets and I counted five diamond rings on her fingers.

"Mrs. Smith, this is my wife, Wanda," John said. "Wanda, this is Grace."

We smiled at each other and I took a chair opposite them. Grace took a cigarette from her mouth and the lipstick was smeared an inch deep on the end.

"John has told me quite a bit about you," she said with a pleasant smile. "You *are* experienced, aren't you?"

"I spent three months at Blanche's," I said. "I don't know if you know her or not."

"Very well," Grace answered. "Would you please show me what you have to sell?"

I stood up and took off every stitch I had on. Naked, I walked over to her and stood with my hands on my hips and kept my eyes fixed on the wall. Grace let the cigarette dangle from the corner of her mouth and turned her head to one side so the smoke wouldn't blow into her eyes. She ran her fingers over my body, beneath my breasts and between my legs. She was making certain that I wasn't a hop-head and wasn't concealing the needle marks. She dropped her hands to her lap as a signal that she was through.

"John, you have a very attractive wife," Grace said. "If she handles herself right, she ought to earn you plenty of money."

John nodded his thanks and gave me a pleased look. I remembered the day that Blanche had told him the same thing. Grace snuffed out her cigarette, a thoughtful expression on her face.

"Would you mind leaving us alone for awhile?" Grace asked him. "Wanda and I have some things to talk about."

John frowned with suspicion and shot me a quick glance. He rubbed his hand against the sofa arm and rolled his shoulders.

"I'll walk down to the corner and get a beer."

"Fine," Grace smiled at him.

She waited until she heard the elevator descending, then she looked at me.

"Honey, how old are you?"

"Eighteen," I paused, "next month."

"What do you know about John?"

I shrugged my shoulders. The girls at Blanche's had told me plenty about him, but her question gave me an uneasy feeling and I felt the crimson rise to my face. I wondered how much she knew about him, or me.

"John's a pimp—a professional pimp. You know that, don't you?" Grace asked. "Don't you know he's only making a fool out of you?"

I swallowed hard at the lump in my throat and felt my hands turn sweaty. I became ashamed of my naked body and I slipped my robe on. I wanted to ask her if it was any of her business how we chose to live. If I didn't mind hustling for him why should she? It was like what John had said before he took me to Blanche's. Why should he work when I could earn more in one night than he could in a week?

John liked nice things. He wanted to wear good suits and drive a new car and he didn't want me going around dressed like Apple Mary. Nice things cost dough and putting me in a whorehouse was an easy way of getting it. But I couldn't tell her that.

"You're not the first girl he's put on the turf and you won't be the last. In a few years, you'll be sharing him with sister-in-laws and when you are all played-out, he'll dump you for a new one," Grace continued. "Honey, you're too nice a girl for this kind of life. Why don't you quit now while you can?"

I shook my head and burst into tears. I hid my face in my hands and my body was racked with sobs. It wasn't true. John loved me. He'd never toss me out and I'd never have to share him. I tried to stop crying and I wondered how I could explain this to her. When I rubbed my hands across my eyes and looked at her, tears were running down my cheeks.

"You don't understand about John or me," I sobbed. "It—it's not like you think at all. If you don't keep me, John will just put me in another whorehouse. Maybe, it won't be as nice as yours."

"How do you know it *is* a nice joint?" she asked. "Did John tell you that?"

I nodded. I couldn't help it, I started crying again. Grace didn't say anything, she just looked at me with a thoughtful expression.

"It's a nice house and you'll like it," she said finally. "Tell John to bring you there about noon tomorrow."

She left without saying another word. I guess she must have known that John would have left me if I had said no. I didn't know she was gone until I heard the elevator. I hurried to the bathroom and washed my face. I hoped John wouldn't be able to tell that I had been crying; I didn't want him asking questions or finding out that Grace had tried to persuade me not to hustle. He might not let me hustle for her if he knew that.

John returned in an hour, the smell of stale beer on his breath. I was in the kitchen, cooking the last of the hamburger.

"Tomorrow night, we'll eat at the Black Angus—a big, thick, juicy steak," John promised. He glanced around the room, "And I'll start looking for another apartment—this crappy joint!"

My crying session with Grace had left me weak and feeling blue, but with John back, I felt better. He was beginning to act and talk like himself again, more like the guy I had fallen in love with and married almost a year ago. If I had it to do over again, I still would have said yes. After I washed the dishes, John counted his change.

"I've got enough for a show," he said.

"Let's go."

Our apartment was just four blocks from the downtown district and we walked. For the first time in a long time, John held my hand. The movie was a light comedy and it snapped me out of the blues. Going home, we walked slowly and window shopped. I saw so many things that I wanted to buy, for myself, for John, and for our apartment.

"Wonder how much I'll earn at Grace's," I asked, casually.

"Couple hundred a night, at least."

"Gosh, that much?" I looked at him with pleased amazement. It didn't sound possible. The highest that I ever made at Blanche's in one night had been a hundred and fifty dollars and for that, I had to hustle seventy men.

"Ten bucks a throw and her girls have 20 to 30 dates a night," John shrugged.

I was used to a lot more dates than that. We walked on home and that night, I slept like a log.

CHAPTER TWO

WOKE UP EARLY and left John still asleep while I packed a suit-case to take with me. I couldn't believe that prostitution was wrong, and getting ready to go to a brothel didn't seem any worse to me than for some other woman to go to work in an office or store.

I guess I'd been pretty dumb about sex when I married. I was so green I didn't even know that prostitution was consid-ered shameful until I had been on the turf a couple of weeks. I guess the worst shock was when I learned that in many cities, prostitutes are treated like criminals. While I was at Blanche's, I hadn't wondered much about it, but since I left her place, I read everything I could find about prostitution.

I read magazine stories that supposedly were written by ex-prostitutes. Some of them were so far from the truth, they seemed ridiculous. In one story, the woman told about the hor-rors and shame of the brothel she had been in. As I read it, I kept wondering what was so horrible about it. The cat house that she described would have been heaven compared to Blanche's.

In other articles, I found some pretty wild errors. Especially the ones that told how women had been forced into brothels and robbed of their earnings. The girls I knew at Blanche's were there because they wanted to be there and, believe me, we earned plenty.

I read every book in the library on the subject, trying to find out why I had been willing. I felt I had found the answer. My parents never told me about sex and I got my ideas about prostitution from John. But it still didn't explain my willingness to return or why I liked being a prostitute.

The books often spoke of the shame. At Blanche's, I had been shamed and ridiculed when I went out in public, but there had never been any shame in offering myself to a customer. I was embarrassed my first two nights, but it was the same embarrassment that I felt on my wedding night. On both occasions, I had been afraid, but I still wanted to go through with it. At Blanche's, I was willing because I was curious to find out what it would be like with other men.

When I left Blanche's, I thought that John would try to put me in another brothel and the idea didn't bother me. I knew what the men would do to me and what they would expect from me. My ignorance of the facts could have been an excuse for my first time, but I couldn't use it now.

About ten, I started to wake John. He was sleeping and he looked so peaceful, I didn't have the heart to wake him. When I kissed him on the cheek, he stirred, rolled over on his back, and flung his arm across my pillow.

John is ten years older than me. He's tall, thin, and has jet black hair and brown eyes. John's hands are large and his long tapering fingers make people think of a piano player. I had always hated a mustache on a man until I met John.

Grace lived in Parkville, 40 miles from us. I carried my suitcase to the bus station and used the last of our money to buy my ticket. I didn't even have enough left for a pack of cigarettes.

I took a seat beside a window and watched the passengers get on. A woman about twenty-five took the seat across the aisle from me. She was tall, slender, and had blue eyes and light brown hair. Briefly, her glance touched mine. There was something in the look she gave me that made me suspect she was a chippy and I wondered if she knew that I was.

I hoped she'd be able to tell so we could sit together and talk, but if she knew about me, she gave no sign, keeping her head turned, staring thoughtfully out the window. I watched her light a cigarette and impatiently smoke it. She would take a long drag, flip the ashes off with her forefinger, and inhale again. In a moment, the floor around her was gray with ashes.

She looked up whenever a man got on the bus, gave him a fleeting glance, then turned her face. I was sure she was a prostitute. I had the same way of looking at men myself. I look at them, not with desire, but wondering if I've done business with them. It's a funny feeling, to look at a man's face that is almost familiar and not remember if you've gone to bed with him or not.

The bus was filled and the driver was in his seat when a soldier, a sergeant, got on. He had his choice of two seats, the one beside me or with the other girl. He studied us both and when the bus started moving, he sat down beside me. I wished he had taken the other seat because I knew he would try to start a conversation, and I didn't want to answer any questions.

We got out of town and the bus started rolling real fast with its funny swing-swing motion that always puts butterflies in my stomach. I can take a bus for a short trip, but on a very long one, I get travel sick. The soldier took out a pack of cigarettes and lit one. He held the pack out to me.

"Cigarette?"

I wanted to say no. If I took one, we'd start talking and I didn't feel like talking, but I took one anyway and watched his face when he lit it for me. He had a nice face. Not handsome or real good looking the way John was, but he had a nice face. I noticed how the crows feet around his eyes wrinkled into a smile when he blew out the match. It's funny, I thought, this is the first guy that I've ever compared to John. I glanced out the window to keep him from reading my thoughts and waited for him to ask me how far I was going.

"If you'll look over there, you can see the only covered bridge left in the state," he said, pointing out my window.

I looked down the gravel side road. The wood bridge spanned a narrow creek. If a horse and wagon had been coming through, it would have looked like a painting.

"It's beautiful, or can a bridge be beautiful?" I asked.

"I think so, especially that one," his slight laugh was slow and easy. "My grandfather helped build it. That used to be a plank road, by the way. The bridge is still pretty sturdy but I don't think it would hold up a heavy truck. Cars use it all the time."

I glanced at him with interest. He had a quiet voice.

"Are you kidding me? I mean about your grandfather?"

"I'm afraid not," he smiled and shook his head. "My grandfather built a lot of bridges. In his later years, he built them out of stone and iron and a good many of them are still standing. But I like this covered bridge the best and I visit it all the time."

He was proud of his grandfather and I thought what it would be like to have grandparents or parents that I could be proud of. I never knew my grandparents, but I was always ashamed of my father. We talked on; Tom Sterling, he told me his name, had a way of raising my interest in little trivial things.

"Who do you know in Parkville?" he asked.

It was a bombshell that caught me by surprise. I tried to think of something to say.

"I—I'm going to see—see about a job," I stammered, "at—at the telephone company."

It was the first thing that popped into my mind. Tom gave me a quick look and tapped out his cigarette with his toe. Next, he was talking about something else, but I was too rattled to make any sense out of what he was saying. I was too thankful that he hadn't asked me anything else and afraid he would.

"I'm stationed in Parkville, but my home is in Amity—that's about thirty miles from here," he said.

"Oh," I answered. Once more I held my breath.

He didn't ask anything else. The bus slowed up and started to rumble down Parkville's brick streets. I watched the street signs, trying to locate Green street. It was eleven-thirty when we pulled into the depot. It was dirty and grimy; the floor and benches were littered with newspapers and empty pop-corn bags.

Tom stayed close to my side, although I tried to lose him in the crowd. I stopped on the sidewalk and drew a sharp breath. I didn't want him following me. He started to take my arm, but I drew away, and he dropped his hand to his side.

"I'm the recruiting sergeant here and I'm in the post office building on Monday, Wednesday, and Fridays," he explained.

"Oh." It was all that I could say.

Just talking to him made me tongue-tied. I didn't like the way he kept looking at me and I wondered if he knew I had lied to him. I was afraid to move. I had told him I was going to see about a job, but I didn't know where the telephone company was. Somehow, it was important that he didn't find out about me.

"I had a very pleasant journey and I hope we meet again," he said.

He turned on his heel and walked away. I waited until he turned the corner and then I followed to make sure that he didn't double back. When I saw him going up the post office steps, half-way up the block, I returned to the depot.

Grace had given me her phone number and I used my last dime to call her. As the phone was ringing, I read the information on the plate above the mouthpiece and found out why Tom had looked at me so strangely. There was no telephone exchange in Parkville. The office was in the adjoining city. Grace answered on the fifth ring.

"Hello, this is Wanda. I'm at the bus station."

"Be there in ten minutes," Grace promised.

She sounded pleased. I waited on the bench that faced the street, thinking about Tom. Now that he was gone, I wished I had told him I was a chippy and where he could find me. He was a nice guy and I would like to have done business with him. But I'd probably do business with a lot of nice guys and a lot more who wouldn't be so nice, so it shouldn't make any difference. He was just a guy I met on the bus.

But it did make a difference. I didn't know why, but I wanted to give in to him and I wondered what he'd say if I had told him I was a chippy. Maybe if he had known that, he wouldn't have been so friendly.

Grace pulled up in front.

CHAPTER THREE

GRACE WAS ALL SMILES when I got into the car, and she chatted about one thing and another as we drove through the downtown traffic. When we bounced across the railroad tracks, she made an abrupt right turn onto a narrow side street. She drove one block and made another right turn. The street was narrow, and the sidewalks lined with huge shade trees.

"I'll show you the red light district first. Then if you want to, you can back down," she said. She slowed up and pointed towards a two-story, white frame house. "That's my place there."

It had a wide porch across the front and one side, and I saw a girl sitting at one of the windows. It was the second house from the corner and a large neon sign on the porch read GRACE. The sign was about a foot high and two feet long. I counted similar signs on ten different houses: BLANCHE, IDA'S, MILDRED'S, and so on. One house had a sign that just said GIRLS. On other houses, there were crude signs on the front porch or screen door that read: PRIVATE, or THIS IS A PRIVATE HOME. I noticed that Grace had a small neon sign above the door: WELCOME.

Girls lounged in the windows, reading, smoking, or just staring at the street. Many of them were scantily dressed, and peering in the windows, I could see other women sitting in the parlors.

"I guess this is the largest red light district in the state," Grace said. "The houses stay open 24 hours a day, the girls work in shifts, and each joint keeps from one to nine girls."

"How many do you keep?"

"Five, six with you, but I imagine a couple of my girls will be leaving before long," Grace answered. "Most of them don't stay too long."

We drove to the end of the block and turned around. Grace drove even slower. I thought she was going to stop, but she sped up when she passed her place. I felt a tinge of fear and disappointment; maybe she was going to send me home.

"Well, Honey, what about it?" she asked. "You still want to hustle for me?"

"You know I have to. John won't give me any peace until I do."

"You could leave him."

"No, I'd rather hustle," I shook my head. "I love him too much to ever leave him."

"What are you going to do when John brings home a sister-in-law?" Grace smiled at me. The thought made me angry.

"I'm an only child and so is John. There will be no sister-in-laws," I answered firmly.

"I said that once, but when my old man brought home another chippy, I was almost glad," Grace said. "You change your mind about a lot of things after you've been on the turf a few years."

She was silent for a few blocks and we were still headed towards the main part of town. Every so often she'd look at me, as if she was still trying to decide.

"O.K. I guess. If you want to hustle for me, I'll let you. You know what it's all about so you can't say you haven't been warned," she said.

"I'll treat you O.K. if you behave yourself and if the customers like you," Grace continued. "I try to treat my girls the way I wanted to be treated when I was a chippy. But keep yourself clean and be nice to the men. I won't keep a girl with a lazy bottom.

Just remember that the men who come to my joint work hard for their money and when they spend it on you, do your best to show them a good time."

I promised her I would. She parked in front of a large downtown hotel.

"Let's go see a friend," she suggested. "By the way, how are you fixed for money?"

"I haven't even got enough for a pack of cigarettes," I answered.

"I figured that. Well, you can ride the bed springs for fun for the next couple of weeks," Grace laughed. "It costs money to be a prostitute in this town."

We took the elevator to the third floor and Grace knocked at one of the rooms. A bald-headed man of about forty answered. He was short, with a large belly, and a red face. He had a frustrated look on his face like a fat man who had just broken a shoe lace on a crowded subway.

"Hi, Bill," Grace said breezily.

She swept on past him and sat down on the sofa. I glanced around. It was a luxurious four or five room suite. Grace smiled at him, yet I could see the scorn and disgust in her eyes when she looked at him.

"Wanda wants to join the union," she said.

Carelessly, she flicked her ashes onto the plush rug. Bill licked his lips nervously and squinted at me.

"She looks awful young," Bill's glance went from me to Grace. "Is she from here? Are you sure she's all right?"

"She was born a whore and she knows the ropes," Grace answered. "That's all you need to know about her."

Bill grunted. He went over to the desk and started writing. The scratching of his pen raked the room. He handed me a receipt for a thousand dollars.

"You sure she's O.K.?" he squinted at Grace again. "She looks awful young."

"Bill, men like them young," she said. "If they wanted them old, do you think I'd be a Madame?"

With a disgusted motion, she threw her cigarette into the ash tray. She dug into her purse and gave him ten one hundred dollar bills.

"See you next month," Bill said to me.

Bill was still holding the money when Grace walked out. She didn't say a word until we got into her car.

"Hang on to that receipt. You have to have it to hustle," she said. "Bill might come around and say that you didn't pay him."

"Who is he, anyway?"

"Just a fall guy and he knows it," Grace answered. "He collects the take from the houses. If anything ever goes wrong, Bill takes the rap. He'll be called a vice lord, but all he does is keep books for the right guys."

"Who are the right guys?"

"I've always thought it wasn't any of my business," Grace answered, with a shrug. "It doesn't matter anyway."

"Here's where we pay out more money," Grace said when we stopped in front of the city hall.

"Oh, Hell! Don't I make anything for myself?"

We went down to the basement and into the City Health office. A man was sitting with his feet propped up on the desk next to a bottle of whiskey. He stared at us with bloodshot eyes and almost fell over when he tried to stand up.

"What can I do for you ladies?"

"Wanda wants a health card." Grace gave him a note from my doctor. Yesterday, John made me go to the doctor to be examined for any venereal disease. He hardly looked at the slip.

"Er—health card," he looked at me and gave a silly little laugh. He wrote my name on a card.

Grace gave him twenty-five dollars and I took the card. It said that I was free from all forms of communicable diseases and I could handle food and be an entertainer. So that's what I was, an entertainer.

Our next stop was the police station. Grace breezed through the front door like she had just made the last payment on the building. We went into the office marked VICE SQUAD. Two detectives were sitting at a card table playing rummy and there was a uniformed cop sitting behind the desk.

"Got a new customer for you, Sam," Grace said. The cop looked at me and coughed.

"What in hell are you doing, Grace, robbing the cradle?" he asked. "Send her back to high school. How old is she?"

"She's eighteen marked up to twenty-two," Grace answered. "But don't worry, this little gal has had plenty of experience."

"They all have. One of these days I'm going to have a Madame bring a girl in here who never has hustled before. That'll be the day," Sam said, shaking his head. "We'll have to check this one out, Grace, so you'll have to put her on ice for few days." Sam turned to me, "All right, Sister, your name and the towns where you've hustled and have a record."

"Wanda Lane, Mrs." I said.

"What's your husband's name?" one of the detectives asked.

"John—John Lane," I turned to face him. "We've been married almost a year."

"She's hustled before, you can bet on that," the detective grunted and picked up his cards as if he had lost interest in me.

The cop shrugged his shoulders. He wrote down my name, examined my health card and receipt from Bill. I was fingerprinted, mugged, and my police record started. It listed my occupation as PROSTITUTE.

"That'll be a hundred dollar fine for disorderly conduct," Sam explained. "You're to appear in police court each Monday and plead guilty to that charge. If you're too busy, your husband can bring the fine in for you. Let us know when you change addresses or decide to leave town. Behave yourself, and we'll let you alone."

"Well, Wanda, you're in business now," Grace laughed when we left the station. "Welcome to the whorehouses."

"Thank the Lord," I said, glad the ordeal was over. "Say, how come the cops knew so much about John?"

"He's done time for White Slavery. Honey, you're not the first girl he's put on the turf." Grace gave me an odd glance out of the corner of her eyes. "You probably won't be the last."

I didn't say anything, but I felt like it. I didn't like the way she kept throwing it up to me about John having had other chippies. Sure, I knew that he had dealt with other prostitutes, and had lived off of their earnings, but it was different with me. I had his name on a marriage license and somehow, that made it different. I was only going to hustle for a few weeks, then quit.

Grace put her car into the garage behind the house and we went in through the back door. It led into the kitchen. Originally, there had been about five rooms downstairs, but some of the walls had been knocked out, and a row of cubbyhole bedrooms had been built out of plasterboard. So now there were six bedrooms, a kitchen, and a living room that faced the front, or as we called it, "The Parlor." When Grace took me into my bedroom, I noticed three girls lounging in the parlor.

My room was long and just a little wider than the double bed that stood in the corner. A white metal table stood beside the bed, and there was a straightback wooden chair, a dressing table, and a chest of drawers. The only light I had was a small bed lamp.

There were no windows. Along the wall, there was a built-in toilet and a clothes closet. I peeked into the closet and then I knew why John had put me in Grace's.

Grace sat on the edge of the bed and watched me put my things away.

"Ten bucks a trick, and I get five. Seven-fifty for a half-and-half, and fifteen for a French date. Whatever you knock down extra is yours, you just pay me five for each trick you hustle," Grace said. "And don't go feeling sorry for anybody; you can't afford to in this business. If a guy tries to bargain or doesn't have enough money, tell him you don't cut prices. If I catch you, I'll let you go.

"One more thing, Honey, don't waste the towels. They cost a buck apiece," she added.

"About how much will I earn?" I asked.

"Oh, $200 to $250 a night, easily. It depends on how eager you are to coin money," Grace said. "My girls have been turning forty to forty-five tricks a night. Tonight will be a pretty slow night, though."

"I'm pretty anxious to earn it," I said reflectively. "It costs a lot to keep that man of mine. You know what I mean?"

"I think I do. I've got the same problem," Grace laughed. "Anything else you want to know?"

"How much do I owe you?"

"Oh, about twelve hundred dollars. Don't worry about it, we'll work it out. Why?"

"Well, could I borrow a quarter for a pack of cigarettes?"

"Good Lord," Grace burst out laughing and slapped her leg.

CHAPTER FOUR

G RACE TOOK ME into the living room and introduced me to her girls. Three of them, Janet, Beverly, and Thelma were on the turf. Janet and Thelma were in their early twenties. Both gave me a casual look and said "Hi." Beverly was a lot older, thirty-five, perhaps even older than that.

I sat down on the sofa beside Grace and she explained to me about the hours. All of us had to be here from six in the evening until three in the morning. Those were the heaviest hours. Her joint stayed open 24 hours a day and we were to take turns hustling the light hours. Beverly acted as Madame when Grace wasn't here.

The set-up was a lot different than the one I had left and I wasn't sure if I'd like it or not. At Blanche's, the men paid her and she gave them a little metal disc to give to us. We waited for them in our room.

Here, one of us sat beside the window and when a man went by, we would motion at him. If he came in, Grace would have us line up and the guy could pick the girl he wanted. The girl and the customer would discuss what the guy wanted and prices in her room.

We waited. It's funny about waiting in a cathouse. It's a lot different than waiting for a bus, or a dinner, or when I was at home, for a date to come after me. It's a different kind of waiting, a feeling entirely its own, a special kind of waiting. It's probably the most lonesome waiting in the world.

I remember how I used to wait at Blanche's and this was the same feeling. It makes you feel good when a man does show up because then you're not waiting any more. The worst nights are the ones when they don't show up. It sent me down into the blues when I was at Blanche's. As I sat there beside Grace and waited, I glanced around me.

There was a juke-box against one wall and I watched the colored bubbles rise to the surface of the tubes. There was a cigarette and a coke machine in the hall. Janet was sprawled out in a chair, idly turning the pages of a movie magazine and Thelma was staring out the window. The clock on the mantel sliced off the minutes like its brass pendulum was a knife.

Thelma leaned forward, smiled, and tapped on the window. I could see the man stop. He looked at her, then at the girl next door, and started up our walk. Thelma walked over, unhooked the screen, and held it open for him.

"Come on in, Honey," she said, smiling at him. "My name is Thelma."

"How much does it cost?" He gave us a brief glance.

"We discuss prices in our rooms, Honey," Thelma said. "You just pick the girl you want a date with. We all charge the same."

"Let's go," he said.

She took him by the arm and led him to her room. Grace motioned for Janet to take the chair by the window. Beverly asked me where I was from and where I had hustled before. I answered her briefly. A couple of guys dressed in work clothes came in together. One took Janet and the other picked me.

"You new here?" he said when I closed the door.

"I just started," I answered. "I've hustled other places though."

He laid a ten dollar bill on the dresser and unzipped his pants. I knew he would be an easy date to hustle. He'd be gentle, the way I liked for men to be.

I put his ten dollars in my shoe and let him have the chair to sit on while he undressed. I pulled off my dress, slip, and panties, and lay down on the bed. There was a shelf on the wall beside the bed. I took down the roll of paper towels and ripped off two to protect the sheet.

There were vacant moments while he finished taking off his clothes. I didn't look at him, but I knew he was looking me over. I thought about the books I had read, about how a woman is supposed to hate prostitution and how shameful it's supposed to be. How women have had to be forced into this business.

Here I was. A nice girl from a respectable family and no one had to force me. I didn't mind doing it with men I'd never seen before, and I didn't mind asking for money. I didn't feel ashamed to do these things or feel ashamed after it was over. I didn't mind having the reputation of a prostitute. I tried to tell myself that there was a reason for all this, but another little voice inside me pointed out that I wasn't the only whore on this street. So I just shrugged my shoulders and reached for the vaseline when he got into bed with me.

I held him close, my cheek against his, and I smiled every time he raised up to look at me. In a few minutes, it was over.

"My name is Wanda, and you be sure and come see me again. If I'm busy—" I wrinkled up my nose at him, "you just wait, will you?"

"Sure, I will," he paused and licked his lips. "Is it all right if I use the back door going out?"

"Sure, Honey," I answered.

I took him into the kitchen and told him good-by again when I let him out the back door. It gave me a funny feeling when he asked to use the back door. He hadn't been ashamed to come in here or to sleep with me, yet he was ashamed that he *had* done business with a prostitute. He had been afraid someone might see him here.

It doesn't make me mad for a guy to tell me that he can't be seen with me or for him to sneak in or out the back way. It just gives me a funny feeling inside. I returned to the parlor.

Now that I had turned a trick I didn't feel so self-conscious in front of the other girls. I got there just as two men were coming in the door. One picked me, the other went with Thelma. My date was almost the same as the first one, except he made a comment on the weather and didn't mind going out the front door. I told him what I had told the first one—my name is Wanda and please visit me again.

When I hooked the front screen door after him, I was the only girl in the parlor. I took a chair beside the window and tried to hook a date, but he shook his head and went into the brothel next door. John drove by. I held up two fingers to tell him how many dates I had turned. He smiled, waved back at me, and drove on.

There was a vacant lot across the street and in it were three parked cars. Four men were sitting on one of the car bumpers.

"There's someone watching the house," I told Grace. She laid down her knitting and peered out the window.

"Pimps—just pimps watching their girls," she said.

Just then I saw John's car pull into the line. He got out and joined the others.

"My old man's over there," I said. "Wonder what they are talking about?"

"Oh, they're probably bragging about how much money their girls earn," Grace answered. "Either that, or trying to decide what cathouse to put her in next."

I felt a little anger. I didn't want John discussing my hustling with pimps. I didn't mind for customers to talk about me, but I didn't want John to.

"He'd better not," I said.

Thelma returned from a date and she put a quarter in the juke-box. It was getting dark and the neon sign on the porch came on. It threw a dusky red light across the porch. Thelma started snapping her fingers and keeping step to the music.

"Gee, I love that tune," she said. When the record ended, she sat down on the sofa beside Grace, stretched her legs out and pointed her toes together. With a bob of her head, she looked at Grace, "What'cha making?"

"Sweater for my new nephew." Grace held it up. It was beginning to take shape.

"Cute," Thelma answered. She tapped her toes together. She walked over to the juke-box, stood there with one hand on her hip, and finally punched the same tune again.

A guy came down the sidewalk and when I pecked on the window, he turned in. I didn't like the looks of his smile when I met him at the door.

"Hi Grace, Hi Thelma," he said in a loud voice. I noticed that Thelma didn't answer his greeting. He looked me over. "Who's the new girl, Grace?"

"Her name's Wanda—this is Sam," Grace answered.

"Yeah, just call me Sam," he threw back his head with a rough smile. "How'd you like to know me better?"

"Fine," I murmured.

He put his arm around my waist and almost dragged me to my room, pinching my bottom as we went.

"I come to the whore houses all the time and just about all the whores are crazy about me. Some of 'em just charge me half price." He looked at me with a gleam in his eye, "You gonna cut your price for Old Sam, Baby?"

"No, I can't do that," I answered. "How do you want it?"

"French Date, Baby, that's how I like it," Sam answered. His face turned serious, "Think you can do it right?"

"I think so." I held out my hand, "Fifteen dollars."

"Hell, Baby, why not ten? Grace won't know what kind of date you give me." He glared at me, "Besides you whores would rather take it that way than you would straight."

"Look, Mister, I don't cut prices for nobody!" I said. Just looking at him made me angry. "Now, if you want to do business with me, O.K. and if you don't, go to one of the other houses."

"O.K., O.K., here's your damn money. You don't need to get sore about it. I was just kidding you. Can't a guy have a little fun?"

"I don't like that kind of fun."

He just belly-laughed, and sat down on the edge of the bed. I knelt down and he grabbed my head so that I couldn't move.

"You dirty whore. You dirty whore," his voice was a raspy breathing. He called me every name he could think of and slapped my face with his open hands.

"Take it easy, Sam," I heard Grace call to him.

I hadn't heard her come into my room. Her warning did some good, but not much. He sat there, rocking to and fro, his chin resting on his chest. He stared at me, a strange look that sent chills down my back. Then his entire body shook and his fingers almost tore out my hair. Slowly, he gave a deep breath and his hands relaxed. I wished I could throw up.

"You did O.K. Baby, you did O.K." His evil smile spread his lips into a toothy grin. "You know, you and me ought to go out sometime, a show maybe. We could have a swell time together."

"No thanks."

"Why not? You don't think you're too good to go out with me!" In a flash, his anger returned. "Maybe you don't know it,

Sister, but there aren't many guys who are willing to go out with a whore like you."

"I got a boy friend."

"Oh, one of those kind," Sam sneered. He slammed my door as he went out.

I waited a few minutes and returned to the parlor. My head still hurt from his hair-pulling and my face stung from his slaps. Thelma was standing by the juke-box.

"How did you and Lover Boy make out?" she asked.

"That son of a bitch," I snapped. "I wish I could have ruined him for life!"

"Wanda, you can watch your language," Grace told me. "This is a respectable place of business and swearing isn't allowed."

Within the next hour, I turned two more tricks. They were just trips to my bedroom. Grace's other two girls came in, laughing and giggling when they turned up the walk. Grace kept her black book in her lap and worked on the sweater. Whenever one of us had a date, she put a check mark beside our name. About nine, we settled with her. I paid her for twelve trips, hid sixty dollars in my closet and kept out the rest for change.

Around ten, Grace finished her sweater and turned her black book over to Beverly and went to bed. Beverly had several dates, but I noticed that she didn't mark them down. She was knocking down and I wondered if I should tell Grace about it, but I decided not to.

About one, business started slowing up and I noticed that a couple of the houses had turned off their signs. Beverly told me that I could quit anytime I wanted to. I was ready. Dog tired from being up so long, I walked up to the corner and stood under a street lamp until John picked me up. I could smell the beer on his breath when I got into the car. He leaned over and kissed me. We had only been apart a few hours, but it seemed like years.

"How'd it go?"

"O.K. I guess. I made enough for our supper."

"Yeah, and how much more?"

I just smiled and shrugged my shoulders. It gave me a kick to keep him dangling and I decided to make him work for the information he wanted. We drove out to a little roadside cafe and had dinner. We sat in the rear booth and I stared at every man that came in. I was afraid one of them might be a guy who I had taken on.

"Trade places with me," I whispered.

John traded seats with me and I sat facing the wall. The men coming in or sitting at the counter couldn't see my face, and I didn't feel so self-conscious. As soon as we got back into the car, I stretched out and went to sleep. John had to shake me awake when we reached our apartment.

CHAPTER FIVE

JOHN LET ME SLEEP late the next morning. When he brought me my breakfast, he sat on the edge of the bed and his hands trembled with excitement as he asked me about my first night at Grace's.

"Did the guys treat you O.K.?"

"Most of them," I shrugged my shoulders. "I had a couple of smart alecs who tried to give me a bad time."

"I guess most of the guys who go to the whorehouses are pretty nice guys," John said. He stuck a cigarette in the corner of his mouth and let it dangle. "For a lot of them, that's the only way they can lay a dame, you know it?"

"I guess so."

"Heck, it's not any worse for a girl to work in a whorehouse than it is a cafe. Anyhow, I don't think so," John explained. "Do the guys ever ask you any questions—you know—about where you're from or if you're married, or anything?"

"Oh, some do. But most of them aren't that interested in me. Some of them will ask me why I'm a prostitute, then I tell them that I'm just lucky or that I need the money."

John threw back his head and laughed, but I couldn't see anything funny. He lit a cigarette and gave it to me.

"I had a couple of guys who wanted to stay all night with me," I said. "They offered me extra to stay in a hotel with them."

"Nothing doing!" John's face grew sober and anger sparkled in his eyes. "You ain't sleeping with no damn customer and I'd better not catch you taking on a man outside a whorehouse. If you know what's good for you, you won't do it either."

"What difference does it make?"

John stood up and stalked across the room. At the window, he turned to face me, his hands knotted into fists.

"It makes plenty of difference. Guys like that would like to steal the factory," John shook his fist at me. "Baby, if I ever catch you stepping out on me, I'll knock your teeth down your throat."

He was jealous and his rage scared me. He stood there glaring at me, his fists shaking.

"Maybe I ought to put you back in Blanche's," he snarled. "You didn't have time to get friendly with the customers there."

"Honey, I'm not getting friendly with anybody. You know me better than that. Honest, you're the only guy I care about."

Gradually, he cooled off and came slowly towards me. I felt my weight press against the pillow and I was scared. I expected him to hit me, but he sat down and put his arms around me, his head lying on my breast. I put my arm around him and patted his shoulder.

"I couldn't stand to lose you, Wanda."

"What about the other prostitutes you've lived with?" I whispered. He shook his head.

"They were chippies before I met them and they never meant anything to me." John looked up at me, an odd expression on his face. "You're the only one that I loved enough to marry. I couldn't stand it if you left me."

He lay there, his eyes closed and not saying anything. For that moment, it was as if I had never known any other man and there was only John. I loved him. I loved him as much as a woman could love any man. Perhaps more, because I loved him enough to swallow my pride and do what he had asked me to. I was a prostitute because he wanted me to be one and I loved him too much to say no.

On our way to Grace's, John drove with one hand. He kept his other arm around me and when we came to a stop light, he would bend over and kiss me.

"Don't take any wooden nickels," he said when he parked in front of Grace's.

He put his arms around me and kissed me again. It made me smile to see him out of his black mood and joking again. He had a way of teasing me about my customers and his remarks always made me giggle. I hopped out of the car and hurried inside. John drove around the block and parked in the vacant lot. There was another car there and the man got out of it and into ours. As I sat down, I wondered where the guys would wait in cold weather.

The mornings are slow and the houses pretty quiet. In the few days that followed, I learned the routine and a few things about Green street. Each morning, the laundry man would stop at each brothel. We rented the cloth hand towels that we used on customers and he charged us a buck apiece for them. I kept seven dozen on hand and generally I would take three dozen one morning and four the next. The towel racket was probably the best money-maker on the street and no other laundry trucks stopped at the houses.

This morning, two plainclothesmen from the vice squad visited each brothel. They shook hands with me and I left a twenty dollar bill in their palms. Grace had told me how much to give them. I saw them on their way back to the station; their pockets bulged with money.

Shirley and I generally hustled the same shift and we were becoming close friends. She was twenty-three and had been on the turf for two years. Shirley was hooked up with a big-time pimp and, as she jokingly put it, she was sister-in-law number three.

I liked it at Grace's; it was so much better than Blanche's had been. The beds were softer and I didn't have broken springs poking me in the back. At Blanche's, I had a bare cubbyhole with plain unpainted walls that seemed to glare at me. I like a room that is tastefully decorated, but I guess the real difference between a five and ten dollar joint is the amount of time you spend with the men. Here, we could give them time to take off their shoes and that made it a lot easier on my shins and really saved on nylons.

I divided my customers into three groups and I could tell by the way a man talked, his actions, and what he said, just what group he was in.

The first group was the "steadies." The guys who visit brothels frequently, but don't always pick the same girl. They're the easiest to do business with. They know the score and in the bedroom, it's all business. They're only interested in getting a kick and many of the "steadies" don't even bother to ask my name. They have a set pattern of sex, and they seldom change or ask to do it another way. Some of these guys like to abuse a chippy and they can get pretty rough. There were plenty of times that I had to grit my teeth against the pain.

The second group is the "straying husbands" brand of patrons. In a lot of ways, it's hard to do business with them. Many of them are just out for a fling and they haven't visited many brothels. They are used to their wives or girl friends and they try to make us like their women are. Most of the guys are a lot more curious about chippies than in going to bed with us.

They ask all kinds of questions and try to get acquainted with us. This is the hard part for me because I don't want my customers to know very much about me and it's pretty dangerous for me to get too friendly with a customer, especially with John watching the brothel. He can see into the parlor and time my dates. If I stayed in my room too long with a guy, he would ask me about it.

I'm ashamed to have customers find out anything about me, like where I came from, what my father does for a living, or how long I've been hustling. At Blanche's, I learned to keep quiet about being married. Guys would always look at me so funny when I told them I had a husband. I try to keep aloof from my customers and fend off their questions with a joke, a quip, or a shrug of my shoulders.

I learned to be careful about telling a customer how many dates I've had or the most men I've ever taken on in one night. If a guy asks, I tell him thirty or forty or whatever number pops into my head. He gets a kick out of hearing it and thinks he's doing me a favor. But if a guy asks me this after he's through with me, I won't tell him. I made that mistake a couple of times and the disgusted look on their faces wasn't easy to take.

Some guys think it's funny for a girl to be in a whorehouse. They never stop to think that we're here for their benefit and not ours. Depending on the guy, I either tell him I'm in business for the fun of it or that I need the money.

"I'm just like lunch meat—always ready," I'll tell some of my customers and they'll laugh. It makes them feel better and enjoy me more.

In secret, I envy the men who come to me. I've often wished that I was a man so I could go to a whorehouse, show a chippy a rough time, and enjoy sex every time I did it.

Most guys believe me when I tell them I'm a chippy because I enjoy sex or that I need the money, but neither answer is true. The money isn't as important to me as men think it it. I gave every dime I earned to John. If I needed or wanted something, even down to a pack of cigarettes, I'd ask him to buy it for me.

Somehow, I felt that the money wasn't mine and it rightfully belonged to John. If I spent any of it without asking him first, it would be like stealing.

The third group that we have to deal with is the "sex perverts," "the degenerates" and so on; men who can't obtain sexual satisfaction from normal sexual relations. It would be impossible to tell the different ways they have used me for their thrills. So many of them are "flaggists" and they love to beat a woman or have her beat them. At Grace's, we had one or two calls a week for a "spanking" and Beverly generally took them.

I broke my rule about getting friendly with customers. I had a real swell guy date me. He was about fifty and his wife had passed away a few months before. He was really a lost soul and I could see the silent misery in his eyes. He looked at me with surprise when I undressed and lay down on the bed. He wasn't used to being with a chippy and he didn't know that here there was no love-making or no build-up to the sex act.

"Take off your bra," his voice was kind. "Please."

"No."

"O.K." he answered and he had a funny expression on his face.

He wanted to take his time and make it last as long as possible, and I let him hold back on me as long as I dared. I didn't want to hurt his feelings by telling him to hurry up. When he finished, he lay still, not moving or saying anything, just holding me close. I could hear his breathing in my ear.

"Get up, Honey," I whispered. "There's others waiting for me."

He got up slowly and started putting on his clothes. He wanted to talk to me in the worst way. I put on my slip and sat down on the bed. He was sitting on the chair, lacing his shoes.

"May I ask you a question?" he asked. "Why wouldn't you take your bra off?"

"It helps protect me. Some guys like to treat me pretty rough and twist my breasts—a bra gives me a little protection."

"It's hard to believe," he shook his head. "I can't imagine any man wanting to hurt a woman."

"Plenty of them do," I shrugged my shoulders. "Some guys ride me like I was a tractor back on the farm."

The guy chuckled.

"Honey, you don't know the half of it," I continued and pointed towards the door. "Notice there's no latch on the door knob? That's in case I need help, I can yell. The guy can't block the door from the inside and the Madame can get in here fast."

The guy looked at me with interest, only it was a different kind of interest than most men have. I felt he understood me.

"That's also why I don't take off my shoes—a spike heel is an effective weapon. If I'm flat on my back, I can twist my leg around and get my shoe. You can really bang a man on the head with a spike heel."

"Does—does this happen very often?"

"Too often," I shrugged my shoulders.

"Why are you a chippy? You don't enjoy sex."

"What makes you think I don't?" I felt the crimson rise to my face and I grinned at him.

"You were pretending. I could tell."

"I guess I never have enjoyed it. I've done it with a lot of guys and I never have enjoyed it. There are guys I hate doing it with and there are guys I like to do business with. You know what I mean?" I made a motion with my hands. "I mean I like them and I want them to have a good time."

"What about me?"

"I like you and I hope you'll visit me again," I paused. I was sticking my neck out. "If you come early in the morning, we can spend more time together—talking."

He looked at me for a moment and my eyes dropped to the floor.

"You must be awful lonely," he said.

He patted me on the leg and went out. I put on my dress and returned to the parlor. Grace looked up from her sewing.

"What in blazes did you two do—go out for coffee?"

"We—we were just talking."

"Well, do your visiting someplace else. You're here for one thing only and I'm not keeping you just to stand and visit with one guy."

"I—I was just trying to be nice to him."

"Just get rid of them as fast as you can so you'll be available for the next guy," Grace snapped. "It costs money to keep this place open and I can't afford to let you waste a half hour with just one customer!"

I didn't answer back because I knew I would only catch more hell. I sat beside the window, watching the street. Pretty soon, I looked over at Grace and said: "I'm sorry. I didn't stop to think."

"Just keep your loving on a cash basis and you'll be all right," Grace answered. "I'm telling you that for your own good. The less you say to a man the better off you are. You don't know these men or anything about them, so it's best not to take any chances."

She was right and besides, I wasn't being fair to her. She couldn't make any money off of me if I let some guy tie me up for very long.

Two days later, the same guy came back to see me. But he came early in the morning when I wasn't very busy. Just Shirley, Grace, and I were there.

"Knock if you need me," I told Grace when I took my friend into my room.

He paid me for a date, but we didn't do anything except to sit on the bed and talk. We had seen the same movies, liked the same kind of music, and had a lot of things in common. The one subject we avoided was sex. That was one of the things that I liked about him. I heard a man in the parlor ask for "Wanda."

"Wait in the kitchen for me," I told my friend, then I pulled off my dress and slip so it wouldn't look funny.

I let him out of my room and motioned for the second one to come in. He had visited me a couple of times before and told me his name but I couldn't remember it.

"Did I interrupt anything?" he asked.

"No, Honey, he just put me in the mood. I'm glad you came along."

I could hardly wait until he was through and had left. I wanted to talk to my friend again, and when he returned to my room, he had a sheepish expression on his face.

"We'd better do it while we've got the chance," I told him.

"Do you want to?" he asked. "I mean if you don't, it'll be O.K. with me."

I gave him a funny look. If he didn't go to bed with me, it would hurt my feelings, make me feel that he thought he was too good for me, but I didn't know how to tell him this.

"Honey, you paid for the date, so you might as well take it," I said. "Come on, let's get it done before I get another call. I'll even take off my bra for you."

I stripped off everything.

"Is this how you want me?" I asked. I put my arms around his neck and pressed my body close to his. I whispered, "I like doing it with you, you're real nice to me."

Afterwards, we sat in the parlor and talked. When a customer turned up the walk, my friend slipped out the kitchen door. Somehow, he didn't like to see me take another man into my room. I didn't think anything about it, but he did.

CHAPTER SIX

PARKVILLE HAD A LOT of steel mills and other heavy industries. When they shut down, our business dropped too. Grace kept just Shirley, Beverly, and me. The other girls slipped away to other towns.

One night when I got into the car, John slapped me. It snapped my head against the door post and the sting brought tears to my eyes. He hit me again, right in the mouth with his open palm. I tasted blood. He slapped me with his other hand.

"Don't—don't!" I screamed.

He kept on slapping me. I tried to shield my face with my hands, but he only pulled them down and hit me harder.

"Dirty, lousy, cheating whore!" he yelled. "I'll teach you to step out on me."

He jammed his hand into my face and slammed my head against the door post; lights exploded in my head and the pain drove hot knives into my skull. For a moment, things turned black and dim.

"I—I haven't stepped out on you," I cried. "You're the only guy I care about."

My words only made him worse and he slapped me again. I let out a scream, and a couple of men walking down the street stopped. When I screamed again, they started towards the car. John jammed the car into gear and we took off, tires squealing against the pavement. When we reached the city limits, John pushed the accelerator to the floor boards. The headlights cut crazy swaths through the darkness as we swept around curves and passed everything on the road. I could see his jaw muscles tensing with anger.

"I—I haven't been cheating on you," I stammered. "I've given you every dime that I've made."

"I'm not talking about money. I'm talking about a guy. Some old guy and you have been holding hands in your room."

"Him? Honest, I don't even know his name," I answered. "I was just trying to be nice to him. Honest, he's old enough to be my father."

"Those kind of guys like to steal the factory, too," John growled. "You just give 'em what they paid for. You don't need to get friendly with them."

"I'm sorry," I stammered. "I won't do it any more."

"See that you don't," John relaxed and eased up on the foot feed.

We drove in silence for about ten minutes. I had cut my lip on my teeth and it was beginning to swell. John pulled me close to him. At first I was afraid, but he didn't hit me.

"Honey, I love you too much to lose you," John said. "Do you think I want one of those louses to run off with you? I get scared every time I think about something like that."

"They don't mean a thing to me, honest they don't," I said. "Even the guy you're thinking about. He's just lonely and I felt sorry for him. We were just friends—that's all."

"Well, don't take him on any more."

I leaned my head against John's shoulder. Secretly, I was pleased. It made me feel good to know that John loved me enough to get jealous over a customer. The lights from the dashboard shone on my nylons. They were so pretty. John had bought them for me. He had been kind to me, always surprising me with new clothes, and jewelry. He had wonderful tastes in clothes and he knew how to select colors and styles for me.

Grace, Shirley, and the others were always complimenting me on my dresses and they often asked my opinion about their clothes. I never told them that I really knew very little about clothes; that John bought most of mine. I raised my head and looked at him.

"You remember what you've been asking me? Well, I asked Grace about it and she says O.K. We'll be alone tomorrow."

John gave me a shy grin and hugged me. I got to the joint about eleven the next morning and I could feel my heart pounding with excitement. Shirley was asleep on the sofa, but I woke her when I came in. We spent sixteen hours apiece on the turf, sometimes more, and Beverly just hustled whenever she felt like it.

Shirley rose and stretched, then slumped into the chair beside the window, patting a yawn with her hand.

"Jeez, what a lousy place. I wish my old man would put me in a joint where there's some action. I've only had two dates since you left!"

"Take off whenever you feel like it," I said. "You need the rest."

"It suits me. I just hope the mills start up before long." She leaned back in the chair and stared out the window. "There's a couple more guys going to Margie. Doesn't that broad ever sleep?"

I peeked out the window. Across the street and two houses down, two men were standing on the porch talking to a tall blond. It took me a moment to place her; she was the girl I had seen on the bus.

"If you were as popular as she is, you wouldn't get to sleep either—that girl is a real hustler," Grace said. "She takes on twice as many men as any girl on this street."

"Who is she?" I asked.

"Margie Johnson," Grace answered. "Her old man's doing time for White Slavery. I just wish she was hustling for me."

I had heard men mention Margie, but I hadn't paid very much attention. Shirley changed into a street dress and left. John was waiting in the vacant lot and I motioned to him. He hurried across the street.

"Hi Grace," he said with a nervous little laugh.

She took him into my room and she had a grin on her face when she returned. She picked up her sewing basket and started working. Finally, she gave a little laugh; "These crazy men!"

It was over half an hour before I hustled another date. It gave me a funny feeling to take a customer into my room, knowing that John was hiding in my closet. It was all that I could do to keep my eyes away from his hiding place. In a way, it embarrassed me, yet I like it, and I really tried to put on a show for him. But as soon as the guy was through, I almost beat him out of my room. I hooked two more dates within the next hour and after the third one had left, I couldn't stand it any more. I peeked into my closet. John was sitting on my suitcase. He came out and glanced around the room, his eyes dancing with excitement.

"You really put out for those guys, don't you?" he exclaimed. "That big guy sure wooled you around, didn't he?"

"Which one was that?"

"The last one. The first one acted like he didn't know what the score was."

I started to say something, but I happened to glance down. I looked up into his face and smiled. His face turned red and he fumbled with his hands.

"You really got excited, didn't you?"

"Yeah, I tried not to—I—I thought that I might,—we—," his voice choked up and his eyes sank to the rug.

"You've ruined your pants," I said. "Let me take care of it."

I filled my wash basin and started to get a towel; then I remembered the coat, so I used a paper towel. John stood very still, and I tried to pretend that it had been he who had just slept with me, but I couldn't even begin to choke that pretense down.

I couldn't help but think that this was the first time in almost a year that I was this close to him. He had tried a number of times, but he hadn't been successful. To have relations with a woman only disgusted him and the only way his desire could be satisfied was to watch me with other men.

"It's no use, Wanda, I—I just can't," John shook his head. "Don't you think I wish I could—that I could be like the men who take you on?"

"It doesn't matter, honest it doesn't. We have each other and that's all that matters." I put my arms around his neck and kissed him, "I'm glad you're not like other men."

I waited until he had left before I returned to the parlor. I stared out the window for a moment and started bawling. Grace came over and put her arm around me. I held onto her dress the way I used to hold my mother's. It was a long time before I could stop crying.

CHAPTER SEVEN

I WAS DOWN in the dumps all day and it was hard for me to smile at my customers. When I was alone, tears would come into my eyes. I couldn't help it. I kept thinking about John and how much I wanted him. It was funny, I could do it with any man who came along, but not with the one I really wanted. I turned the juke-box up as loud as I could and kept playing it. It was the only way that I could drive those thoughts out of my mind. I was nervous and my hands were shaky. It seemed that I dropped everything I picked up; objects just slipped out of my hands.

Shirley returned at seven. She looked as fresh as a daisy and she almost bounced into the house. I envied her cheerfulness and I hoped some of it would rub off onto me.

"I heard you got slapped around last night," she smiled at me.

"Who told you?" I snapped.

"Oh, I just heard—men talk you know. I'll bet you won't be getting lovey-dovey with your customers any more," she said. "Here, look, I'll show you something."

She pulled back her dress and slipped her bra down. I looked at her breasts. The nipples were almost gone and covered with scars.

"That's what my old man did when he found me cheating on him. He burned me with a cigar. Boy, did that teach me!" Shirley slipped her straps back on. "You were lucky all you got was a slapping."

"I was just being nice to a guy," I explained.

"What's the use of being nice to a guy?" Shirley shrugged her shoulders. "That doesn't get you any place. They don't pay you extra for it and they won't think any more of you for it. Do you think any of the crumbs that come here would be seen walking down the street with you? Hell no, they wouldn't!"

I moved my shoulders and stared out the window. I wondered if I could make her understand. I didn't care for my friend and that's all that he was—a friend, but I didn't say anything. If I did, it would be carried to John and I'd have to answer for it.

My friend didn't come around for a couple of days and I had almost forgotten him until I saw him coming down the street one morning. John was across the street and there wasn't much I could do.

"Hello, Wanda, how have you been?" he asked with a cheery smile.

"O.K. I guess." I stared at the flowers on the wallpaper while he made awkward motions with his hands. He reminded me of a little boy trying to recite a poem. I knew that he was too self-conscious to say anything in front of Shirley and Grace.

"Why don't you go to bed with Shirley?" I suggested. "She can show you a good time."

"I—I was thinking about you," he stammered.

"Oh, give Shirley a break. You've had enough of me," I answered. "I get tired of going to bed with the same men all the time."

He didn't answer, but just looked at me. I would have preferred that he hit me because a beating would have been easier to take than the hurt look he gave me. He didn't even glance at Shirley, but turned around and walked out. I watched him go up the sidewalk, walking as fast as he could and it was all I could do to sit still. I wanted to run after him and tell him I was sorry. I turned my face so Shirley and Grace wouldn't see my tears.

"Boy, wasn't he a stuck-up bastard?" Shirley said. She jammed her hands on her hips, "Who does he think he is—not wanting to go to bed with me."

"Can it!" I screamed and burst into tears.

"Gee, I'm sorry, Kid, I didn't know you cared," she answered. "I didn't mean it—not the way it sounded."

"I didn't care about him—that's the worst part," I said. "It would be easier if I did."

I gripped the chair arms until my knuckles stood out white. I didn't care. I didn't care about anyone—not even myself. I felt cold, hard, and vacant inside; like an old house that no one lives in any more. Of all the men I had "dated," only one had treated me like a woman. But I wasn't a woman and men didn't think of me as one. To them, I was a prostitute, something to buy and paw over, and to leave here until they wanted me again. One guy had been nice to me and had been different, and because he had been, I wasn't allowed to see him any more.

Some guy came down the street and I walked to the door, instead of pecking on the window. I wanted him to know that I was a chippy and I wished we could stand naked on the porches and shout out our wares.

"Come on in, Honey, I'll show you a good time," I called out.

"How much?"

"Ten bucks. Come on, I haven't had a date all morning."

"There's a girl down the street who sells it for five," he jerked his head towards one of the houses down the street.

"She knows what her fanny is worth and I know what mine is worth," I answered. "Would she sell it for five if she could get ten?"

He paused for a moment, deep lines in his forehead. I wanted to go out and drag him in, but I knew Grace wouldn't let me. According to the rules, we weren't allowed to even go out on the porch to solicit. He threw his cigarette away and finally said, "Too much."

He walked on. It made me feel cheap and rotten. I hated him for turning me down. Another man came along and I hooked him. I took him to my room without asking if he wanted to go to bed with Shirley.

"I can put out a good French Date if you want it," I said when I got him into my room. He shook his head.

I laughed when I kicked off my panties and I wanted him to think I was the hottest whore on Green street. I was determined to give him the best ride he ever got from a woman. I had never felt this way before. When he got on top of me, I opened my eyes wide like I was pleased. He didn't tumble to the fact that I was just acting.

That night I took on thirty-four men, the most that I had taken on since the mills shut down. Shirley only turned twenty tricks. When John drove after me the next morning, I handed my money to him as soon as I got into the car. His eyes bugged out with surprise when he counted it.

"What happened to you?" he asked.

I just laughed.

CHAPTER EIGHT

THE FIRST LAWS and commandments concerning marriage and adultery were surely written by women or else women had a strong voice in their making, because prostitution and adultery are not a woman's emotion. Sex is very personal with a woman, a lot more so than with a man. A woman wants to keep house, cook, sew, wash diapers, and watch her children grow up. That's a woman's natural way of expressing her love.

The worst is to realize that you're just a sport for men and you can't do the things you are supposed to do. Although prostitution is a life of ease, luxury, and gaiety, I have my somber moments and I'd gladly trade it for a tub of dirty diapers.

During the next few days, it was hell living with myself. There was a cold fury inside me that made me bold and shameless. I was all smiles in front of my customers, but my smiles were as phony as my passion. Still I fooled the men and I got a satisfaction out of knowing that. I would wake up in the morning hating myself for what I had said and done the night before.

I was nervous, irritable, and it took very little to set my temper off. One morning I got mad at John for some trivial thing he had done and I threw a cold cream jar at him. He ducked it, then stared at me with his mouth open in amazement. The only one who was pleased with my change of character was Grace. She endured my outbursts for the additional money that I brought in.

I took my spite out on both her and John. Yet, I didn't really know what I was mad about. I guess I was just mad at the system. The entire rotten set-up.

To me, there is nothing indecent or wicked about being a prostitute and I don't consider myself a bad girl. Prostitution is shameful only because other people consider it so. I don't mind being a prostitute if I know that I can beat the system. Some girls hustle for awhile and then quit. They've beat the system. Others keep on hustling and hustling, and end up on skid row rotten with disease or else they become Madames—which to me, is a thousand times worse than being a prostitute. I had the fear that I wouldn't beat the system; that I'd live out my days in some crummy whorehouse.

In a few days I calmed down and started acting like my old self again, but I still had that vacant feeling inside me. Before my "mad" spell, I had been very discreet about my activities, but during that week, I had the urge to tell people that I was a prostitute.

Once, I went into a department store in Parkville and approached the lingerie counter. The girl who waited on me was about two years older than me.

"May I help you?" she asked.

"Yes, yes, I need something very nice," I said. I looked at her and tossed my head when I smiled, "to wear in a whorehouse."

It was a moment before she fully realized what I had said. I watched the look of scorn spread over her face as I picked out several items and handed them to her. She wrapped them and took my money, but I noticed how she unconsciously wiped her hands after she put the money in the cash register.

I stopped to look at some curtains. The clerk whispered to another girl, then they both looked at me. Their looks of scorn and disgust hurt me, but I wanted to be punished. I no longer cared if people found out what I was. The better known I became, the more customers I would have. I didn't feel ashamed with a customer and the more men I took on, the less time I'd have to sit and stare at the floor.

The spell left me, dying a little each day. I told myself that I could quit before long and John and I would start our family. Perhaps we would buy a little business somewhere. John had seemed mildly interested whenever I had talked about it.

A few days after I calmed down, John suggested that we try another town. I was doing as well as any of the girls on Green street, but the mills were still shut down and the men didn't have the money to spend on us.

"It suits me. I'm getting tired of this town," I told John. "Just find me a joint where there's plenty of action."

I helped John pack his suitcase. He would make a circuit of the cities that had open prostitution to check out the prices on how much the girls were earning. Then he would try to place me in the brothel where I would earn the most. I looked forward to being in another cat-house. I was tired of Grace's, the same men who came to me, and everything about it.

The second morning after John left, I walked to the bus station to ride to Parkville. I stood beside the door, waiting for the bus to start loading.

"Did you find the telephone office?"

I jumped with fright and looked around. It was Tom Sterling, the soldier I had met on my first trip down. He gave me a shy grin and I felt the crimson rise to my face. I wondered if he knew about me.

"No," I answered, with a nervous little laugh.

The bus doors opened and the people rushed around us. I lost him in the crowd, but he had hold of my arm when the bus driver took our tickets. We sat down together. I remembered how guiltily Margie had looked at the men who got on the bus and I tried not to look at the passengers the same way. But I couldn't help myself. So many of them looked familiar that I wondered if I had gone to bed with them. If the men recognized me, they gave no sign. Tom was talking, but I couldn't keep my mind on what he was saying. I heard only snatches of his conversation and I managed to say "yes" and "no" at the right times.

When the bus started moving, I sank back into my seat. At least none of my steady customers were here or anyone who could cause me trouble. Guys have done that to me plenty of times. I've been walking down the street and men have yelled out things at me so the other people on the street would know I was a chippy. Wise guys.

Tom offered me a cigarette and bent close when he lit it. I liked the feel of his body close to mine and I wondered if he was going to kiss me in front of all these people. He might have been tempted, but he didn't try.

"I've often looked for you," he said.

I looked at him, but his face told me nothing. Apparently, he didn't know about me and had never seen me on Green street. Maybe he was the kind that didn't visit cat-houses.

"I'm staying with a lady," I said.

"Are you a nurse or housekeeper?" he asked.

"Oh, just a housekeeper," I answered.

This wasn't a game that I enjoyed playing. But it was nice to meet a guy who thought I was decent and who wasn't anxious to shove money at me. I relaxed and we chatted all the way to Parkville.

"How about a date?" he stammered as we gathered up our things.

"When?"

"How about tonight? We could go to a show or something."

"I—I'll have to sneak away," I said. "But I think I can arrange it."

"About six?" he suggested. "We'll meet here at the depot."

I said O.K. without even thinking and my heart was fluttering when he left me. I watched his broad shoulders disappear into the crowd and it left me shaky inside. I felt the way I had when a boy asked me for my first date in high school. I took a taxi to Grace's.

The day started out like all the other days, but this one seemed special to me. I kept my eye on the clock and I wondered if Tom would make a pass at me, and what I'd do if he did. The laundry man came by and we debated about how many towels I would need. Since the shut-down, I hadn't been keeping too many and last night I had to borrow a dozen from Shirley. I ordered six dozen and Shirley took three.

"You're doing O.K., Wanda," the laundry man said. "That's how many Margie took today and she always uses a dozen more than any girl on Green street."

"Yeah, but she works around the clock," I answered. "I could coin as much as she does if I did that."

"She's got a deal though. She's her own Madame and she doesn't have to split with anybody," the laundry man continued. "Boy, how I'd like to team up with a broad like that."

"Hasn't she got a pimp?"

"Naw, and she won't have. A guy tried to take her over and she shot him in the hand—a couple of pimps have tried to move in on her. She's different from other whores—you can tell. That dame has a cash register for a heart," he said. "Say, some of the guys around town have been talking about you."

"Yeah, what kind of guys?" I felt myself stiffen. "What do they say?"

"Oh, nothing bad—you know, just guys," he backed up a step. "You know how men like to talk about you girls. I just heard some guys say that you were a first class chippy and that you really liked to put out."

"Maybe I do," I smiled at him. "Why don't you find out? You can take my towel money out in trade."

"I'll give you a whirl one of these days—I've been aiming to. But my wife is hustling across the street and she'd kill me if she caught me going to bed with another chippy."

He picked up his bag of used towels and left. After him, two members of the vice squad came around to shake hands with us. I watched them make the rounds from house to house. After them, the man came to change the records on the juke box. He played a couple and Shirley and I picked the ones we liked best.

About one, someone knocked on the kitchen door. Sometimes a bashful customer will come to the back door. When I answered it, a short, heavy-set man brushed me aside and walked in. He paused by the kitchen table, his hands jammed into his coat pockets.

"You Grace?" he asked. "Joe sent me to collect."

Puzzled, I called Grace. Shirley came following after her. The man looked us over and shrugged.

"Joe said for me to collect ten bucks apiece from you and your girls," he said.

Grace looked at him for a moment, biting her lip. He just stood there, waiting.

"Oh, hell, give it to him," she said.

I took ten dollars out of my shoe and when he took the money, I noticed the word LOVE tattooed on his left hand. One letter to each finger. He didn't even say thanks. We watched him go next door and from there, to the next brothel.

"Who's Joe?" I asked.

"In this business, you don't ask questions," Grace snapped.

Shirley and I returned to the parlor. I was more interested in watching the clock than the street. I couldn't keep my mind off my date with Tom. Two men paused in front of the house.

"You Wanda?" they asked from the sidewalk.

"Sure," I answered. "Come on in."

It pleased me to have men make it a point to ask for me. Shirley retreated to the kitchen before they made it through the door. Neither of them asked Grace if she kept any other girls. While I took one of them to my bedroom, the other waited in the parlor. I was curious as to why they had asked for me.

"We heard a couple guys in a bar talking about you," the guy grinned shyly. "They were bragging about how you could put out and said that you were hotter than a little red wagon."

When he told me that, I just wished that John had been in my closet so he could have heard it. I was becoming notorious as a prostitute. I should have been ashamed, but it didn't even occur to me. I had a couple more customers and around four-thirty I started complaining about a splitting headache.

About five, my headache grew a lot worse and I asked Grace to let me go home. It was a bad time to get off because our heaviest hours are from six to midnight. I don't think I was fooling her any, but about five-thirty she told me that I could take the rest of the night off. I changed clothes and forced myself to take my time. If I appeared too anxious, Grace would make me stay. I called a taxi and it was five minutes after six when I hurried into the depot.

Tom was waiting for me. We had dinner in a small cafe and I felt bad letting him spend his money on me. He made so little and I made it so easy. I probably made more money in one night than he did in a week.

After dinner, we sat in the booth and talked. I told him very little about myself, just where I was born, then I changed the subject. I liked his ideas, his thoughts, and the things he believed in.

We went to a movie and he held my hand. That's all he did. But I couldn't keep my mind on the show or even follow it. The way he squeezed my hand did something to me. It had been a long time since I had enjoyed myself so much.

After the show, we were walking towards the little cafe, when we crossed an alley. He still held my hand. Tom hesitated, his face deadly serious, and he pulled me within the shadows and leaned me against the brick wall.

"Come here," he said gruffly.

He was a little rough with me, the way a guy who is bashful generally is. He stood looking at me. I looked up at him, pleased at his shy smile and the gleam in his eye. He kept swallowing the lump in his throat. He bent his head to kiss me, but I ducked out of his embrace. He didn't try to hold me.

"Take it easy, you're going too fast," I said.

"I'm sorry, I didn't mean—" he fumbled with his cap. "You're not mad, are you?"

"No, Silly, I'm not mad," I laughed. "We'd better be going."

We started on down the street. I left my hand free so he would hold it again. We walked a little ways and it gave me time to think things over. I stopped and looked at him.

"You should always finish what you start," I said.

He backed me into the dark doorway of a store and slipped his arms around my waist. This time I didn't dodge. I closed my eyes and gripped his jacket with my hands when he kissed me.

"We'd better be going," I said. He bent to kiss me again, but I turned his cheek with my hand, "Once is enough."

He laughed. It was a nice laugh. He wasn't angry or anything, and I knew I had let him go as far as I could. I might let him kiss me good-by, I couldn't make up my mind about that yet, but that would be all. If I hadn't liked him so much, I could easily have let him go all the way with me. But I didn't want Tom to think of me as just a pick-up or a cheap tramp. Before he found out I was a chippy, I wanted him to know that I could be a nice girl.

The next bus was at two a.m. We sat in the little cafe until it closed and then sat in the bus station. We made our next date for Wednesday afternoon; that way I wouldn't have to miss the pay hours at Grace's and I knew she wouldn't let me off very many times.

When he started to get on the bus, Tom turned and kissed me. There were others doing the same thing, so I didn't mind. He waved at me while the bus backed out into the street. I just stood there until its lights disappeared. My head was high in a cloud. I had met the most wonderful guy.

It was too late for me to go home and if I went back to Grace's, I'd have to answer questions, so I went to a hotel. I tossed and turned in bed when I dreamed of him kissing me. Once I woke up and had to put the covers back on the bed. I had tossed them onto the floor. The effect that he had on me was frightening and I couldn't understand it. I had never felt that way about anyone, not even John.

CHAPTER NINE

T HE NEXT DAY Grace didn't ask me any questions, except how I was feeling. The guy that Joe sent around showed up again and we had to give him ten bucks. It was a long, dull day for me and my back ached from hustling so many dates. When I quit about one in the morning, John was waiting for me.

Although I hadn't seen him for several days, it didn't please me to have him back. Secretly, I wished he'd never come back because he complicated things with Tom.

"Hi ya, Baby, I really found you a swell joint," he greeted me. "It's a ten dollar house and you'll really have a good time. The other girls are averaging fifty men a night."

"You can keep it. I'm staying with Grace," I answered.

Suddenly, I was mad at him. John gave me a stormy look and drew back his hand as if he was going to hit me, but I didn't flinch. If he hit me, I would hit him back. Instead, he dropped his hand to the steering wheel.

"What's the matter with you anyway?" he asked; surprise in his voice. "I did what you told me to do and now you're sore because I did. You complained about Grace's and now that I've got you set up to earn some *real* money, you say you ain't going."

"That's right, I'm not."

"What am I going to tell the Madame? She's expecting you."

"I don't care what you tell her—tell her anything you want."

"But she's expecting you," John hit the steering wheel with his palm. "You'll be leaving her in a lurch. Wanda, it's a swell joint."

"That's tough. If it's such a nice joint, why don't you take my place?"

John gave me a disgusted look and shut up. I knew he wouldn't say any more about it until we got home and then he would really start in. I didn't even bother to ask him about the joint, I wasn't even that interested. I wouldn't leave Tom. I looked at John and tried to see what had once made me think I loved him. But I couldn't see it now. He was just a guy to me and I felt the same indifference towards him that I felt towards my customers.

"You hungry?" he asked. He was still sore. I could tell by the tone of his voice.

I said yes and we stopped at a night club at the edge of Parkville. It wasn't too crowded. I saw several chippies from Green street sitting in a rear booth, laughing real loud, and having a good time with their pimps. We took a booth near the front. I folded my hands on the table and waited for our order. I didn't even look at John.

Bill, the guy whom I had paid the thousand to when I first started, left the bar and came over to our booth. He pulled a chair from a table and sat down facing us, putting his glass of beer on our table.

"Hi, Kids," he said with a toothy grin. He looked at me and his smile broadened, "I'll be around to see you one of these days."

"Times are hard and it's been rough," I snapped. To me, Bill was just a leech. "You may have to wait on your thousand."

"I guess you haven't heard the latest," he said, still smiling, "The boys have cut the price to five hundred for awhile."

"That's sweet of them," I said. Bill shrugged his shoulders.

"Well, what the hell? They don't want to make it tough on nobody. Business has been slow and you girls have to work for your money just like everybody else." Bill turned his chair towards John, and made a sawing motion with his hands. "Say, that wife of yours is really turning into a first class hustler. She's getting to be the most popular whore on Green street."

John gave me a funny look and his lips went flat against his teeth. He rubbed the top of one hand with the palm of the other.

"The boys have been thinking that she might be able to use a better set-up. You know what I mean?" Once more, Bill made a funny motion with his hands. "They like to give a girl a break and if you want to, we can brag her up a little and throw some business her way."

"You talk to her—it's her fanny," John answered. His face was strangely serious.

Bill gave him an odd look. He turned towards me and swallowed at the lump in his throat. The sweat was glass beads shining on his forehead. I guess he knew what he wanted to say, but he didn't know how to go about it, talking directly to me. He drained his beer glass.

"Are you interested?" he asked.

"What's the deal?"

"The boys just fix it so you earn more money. They've got lots of friends, bar keeps, taxi drivers, and the like," Bill hunched his fat shoulders. "These guys just brag you up and tell guys who might be interested how good you are."

He fingered his beer glass for a moment, making dark circles on the table with it. He kept looking away from me.

"You'll earn plenty—twice what you're making now. But it's a rough go and I wouldn't blame you if you said no."

"Go ahead—that's what I'm in business for—to earn money," I said without hesitating. I didn't even bother to look at John to see how he felt about it.

"I'll tell the boys," Bill said. I noticed that he wasn't smiling. "How about exhibitions and parties? You want to go in for them too?"

"Sure."

Bill left our table without saying anything else. He sat alone at the bar. I thought, sure, I'm low-down and people consider me dirty, but what about guys like Bill? They feed off of whores like me and really, he's lower than I am. I noticed the odd look on John's face. He was just sitting there, staring at me.

"What's the matter?"

"Nothing's the matter," John answered.

"Well, you wanted me to hustle and you forced me to become a prostitute," I snapped. "I thought you wanted me to say yes to Bill."

John didn't answer. He stared off into space and occasionally, he would lick his lips. On the way home, I kept my distance from him. He didn't try to put his arm around me and if he had tried, I wouldn't have let him.

"John, how many men have I done it with?" I asked. He kept a close score. One reason was for our income tax and the second, for his own thrills. He got a kick out of adding them up.

"At Blanche's, about two thousand and so far about three thousand at Grace's," he answered.

He didn't ask me why. Five thousand men. That really wasn't very many, I told myself, and Tom shouldn't care about them because they meant nothing to me. There had been women who had spent twice as long on the turf and then married a decent guy. Their men had forgiven them. I felt sure that Tom would understand.

"Come here, I want to show you something," John said when we reached home.

Reluctantly, I went with him. He led me down the street to where a brand new snow-white Cadillac convertible was parked. He reached into his pocket and handed me a set of car keys.

"You can drive this to work now," he said, grinning.

I dropped my purse. I was too stunned or shocked to say anything. It was the most beautiful car I had ever seen in my life.

"It—It's mine?" I squealed.

"It is if you keep up the payments," John grinned at me.

I threw my arms around his neck and started kissing him. I wasn't mad at him any more and I was so happy I wanted to cry. John finally pulled my arms from around his neck and he practically had to drag me to our apartment. I was so excited that I couldn't sleep and all I could talk about was my convertible.

CHAPTER TEN

NOTHING HAD ever thrilled me as much as that convertible John bought me. To think that it was mine, mine alone, made me weak in the knees. I loved its pure white color and the custom-made leather seats. It had three times as many knobs, dials, and other things on the dashboard as our car. John explained what they were for, but I was too excited to listen. I learned where the switch, gasoline gauge, and the radio were, and I ignored the rest.

The next morning, I bought a fur neck piece and a new dress to match the car. I couldn't wait until I got to Parkville to show it off. I drove up and down the main street, acting real sophisticated when I received cat-calls and wolf whistles from men. When I drove down Railroad street where all the warehouses were, some of the men recognized me and yelled: "Hi, Wanda!" I parked my car in front of Grace's and while I waited for dates, I just sat and admired it. The guy from Joe's came around and nicked us for ten bucks again.

"That guy is really collecting," Shirley commented.

In the afternoon, we heard some good news. The mills were going to start up again, but it would be a couple of weeks before the men would get a paycheck and be able to spend money on me. I didn't tell Grace about my talk with Bill. I thought it better if I let her find out from someone else. If I got to stay with her, she'd really make a lot of money off of me.

I knew what Bill was going to do to me. I'd seen it done to other chippies. In every red light district, there are one or two prostitutes who become better known than the rest. It isn't the beginner who becomes popular, but the gal who knows the ropes and has had the experience to show the men a good time.

In a lot of cases, the fame is due to the chippy's own eagerness to earn money, but part of her fame can come from her pimp or vice lords. It's easier to brag about one prostitute than it is a dozen different girls or the entire red light district. Not only in Parkville, but also in the surrounding cities, my name would be mentioned in bars, taverns, and other places.

A girl's fame lasts until she leaves town or another girl starts taking her customers away from her. It used to be Margie who was so popular and she was the prostitute that men "ought to go visit." Soon, it would be me. That is, if I could live up to the claims that the men would make about me.

I would become the most notorious woman in town and it would be impossible for me to walk down the street and not be recognized. The comics in the night clubs and strip joints would start giving me plugs. They would tell the jokes about me that they were now telling about Margie.

But the satisfaction wouldn't come from the extra money that I'd earn, but the way I would be treated. The other whores on Green street would talk about me, some would envy me. The Madame would treat me like a queen. I was getting a taste of this royal treatment from Grace and I wanted all of it. At Blanche's, her favorite girl was waited on hand and foot and whatever she wanted, Blanche got for her. If she didn't, her pimp did.

I made the men pay. In doing so, I was smarter than the girls who put out and didn't collect. Sure, I knew the dangers of prostitution. The chances of getting diseased, the shame and disgrace, or the dangers of ending up on skid row. But I went to the doctor each week and took very good care of myself. With modern drugs, medicine, and medical knowledge that's available, venereal disease is not the prostitute-killer that it once was.

As for ending up on skid row, I laughed at that. I was smart enough to stay away from drugs and heroin and I wasn't about to become a drug addict or an alcoholic. When I got older, I would simply quit hustling. Meanwhile, I would enjoy the luxuries, the nice clothes, and the other things that I could afford. What could put me on skid row?

As for the shame and the stigma of prostitution, I had that whipped too. I lived in one city and hustled in another. A chippy doesn't feel ashamed of what she does when she's in a cat-house. It's only in certain situations when she feels the shame. I had learned how to duck most of those situations.

Just before I left Grace's that night, Bill called. He said he'd be down the following afternoon to discuss business with Grace and me. Although he didn't say so, the business would be how my earnings were to be divided up. Under the present deal, Grace and I split the ten bucks, but the boys weren't going to handle me for free. I imagined that my earnings would be divided equally between Grace, Bill, and myself. Instead of half, I would get a third, but perhaps I would earn more in the long run.

As I left, I told Grace that I'd be back the next evening and whatever deal she and Bill made would be O.K. with me. I was more concerned about my date with Tom and I wasn't going to break it.

The next day, I left my car in a public garage and took the bus for Parkville. Margie was on the bus when I got on. She was returning from her monthly visit to her husband. The only time she left the red light district was to go up to the prison to see him. She moved over and sat beside me.

"I hear that Bill has turned up your thermostats," she said.

"I guess so," I answered.

"They'll do to you what they've done to me."

"You haven't done so bad. I don't see what you've got to kick about."

"Nothing, I guess," Margie hunched her shoulders. "I asked for it, the same way you have. But if you're smart, you'll get out now while you can."

Her preaching made me mad. I was jealous of her because she was more popular than I was. I knew that she hated me because I had been taking customers away from her.

"So you can still be the favorite?" I sneered.

"No, I'm about through in this town. The men are getting tired of me," Margie answered. "I guess I'll get me a girl and watch her make the mistakes I made. I was just trying to help you."

"I can imagine."

"Honey, they'll teach you what a dirty word 'prostitute' really is," Margie answered. "You'll do things that you'll even be ashamed to tell another prostitute. You're not a prostitute yet. Wait until they get through with you and you'll know what whoring is really like! It's not as easy as you think it is."

Before I could answer, she moved to another seat. Every time I looked back at her, she had her head leaned back and her eyes closed. She was still young and attractive and she could do O.K. in another town. But she had a good deal in Parkville and she didn't want to leave it. She didn't want to give up her customers or become a has-been. In Parkville, she already was a has-been, but she didn't know it.

I knew what some of the men were saying about her. She used to be good sporting but she was all played out. Still, she had plenty to offer the guys and she would be rough competition for me.

I watched her hail a taxi, as if she couldn't wait to get back to Green street. Tom hadn't arrived at the depot yet, so I went up to our little cafe to wait. For my date with Tom, I wore a plain blue suit that I'd had for sometime, and very little make-up.

No one looked at me when I walked up the street. Yesterday, in my convertible, I had raised plenty of cat-calls and whistles. In the rear booth, I ordered coffee and waited. Our date would be in the daylight and there would be little chance for any love-making. I was glad in a way, but it didn't solve my problem. Sooner or later, I knew that I'd let down my barriers and give myself to Tom.

Three men came in and sat down together at the counter. I recognized them as steady customers of mine and two of them had often visited me together. They gave me a brief glance, but none of them recognized me. I lit a cigarette and listened to their talk.

One of them had been to a strip tease act the night before and he was telling the other two some of the jokes he had heard. They were talking so low I heard very little, but I heard him mention "Wanda the Whore" several times. I didn't catch the ending of the joke, but it was something about how many customers I took on.

The men laughed and bent their heads close together. I heard one of them remark: "She's that little brunette at Grace's."

It amused me to hear the men talk about me and not recognize me. Just by changing my hair-do a little, the make-up I wore, and my dress, I was a different person. It gave me a smug satisfaction to know that I could meet my customers out on the street and not be recognized by them.

I saw Tom go past the cafe. I paid for my coffee and I was conscious of one of the men staring at my legs when I went out. They still didn't recognize me. I caught Tom just before he went into the depot. Since he had to catch an early bus, we hurried to the show. At first, he put his arm around me, but people looked at us, so he took it down and just held my hand.

"Wanda, I think you're wonderful," he whispered in my ear. I turned and smiled at him. He bent forward again, "Darling, I could really care for you."

His words thrilled me and I had been wanting to hear him say them, but they also troubled me. There were so many things that I had to tell him—that I was married and was a prostitute. He was starting to get serious. I liked it and I had been hoping he would. But I still had to tell him about myself and in such a way that he would understand.

All during the show, I kept thinking about how to tell him. It was almost six when we got out of the show and we had to hurry to catch his bus. We didn't have much time to talk and I wondered if this was the time to tell him. He said something about my being wonderful again and I said something about him feeding his line to all the women and I dropped a hint about the scarlet women here in Parkville.

"You mean those girls on Green street," he laughed. I felt the color rise to my face.

"I suppose you don't ever go see them?" I kept my face straight ahead and looked at Tom out of the corner of my eye.

"No thanks," he said gruffly and he acted insulted. "I wouldn't be caught dead in one of those places."

"How about alive?" I giggled.

"I said no thanks," he answered. "I don't care to have anything to do with a woman who has that little pride in herself."

The crimson went deeper into my cheeks and the street swam before my eyes. I gripped his hand and tried to think of something to say. I wanted to tell him, but if I did, I would lose him. I had to find a way so that he would understand and wouldn't hold it against me. I didn't want to risk losing his love.

They were loading the bus when we got there. Tom bought his ticket and at the door, took me into his arms and kissed me. I closed my eyes. I had the fear that this might be the last time I would ever kiss him and I tried to show him all the feeling and affection that I had for him.

CHAPTER ELEVEN

W HEN I GOT to Grace's, Bill was waiting out front in his car and my suitcases were sitting on the front porch. He motioned for me to get into the car and he grunted when he put my luggage in the trunk.

"Grace ditched you. She won't keep a syndicate girl," he explained. "Jeez, are we in a spot!"

"Well, I can't do it on the curbing, the neighbors would talk," I answered. "Why don't you fix me up with a set-up like Margie's? Let me rent one of those shacks and hire some woman to keep house for me and act as Madame."

"No dice. The cops say there's too many houses on this street now," Bill shook his head. "They want to close a couple as it is."

"How about letting me talk to the Boss?"

"No."

"Why not?"

"The Boss don't talk to whores, that's why," Bill answered.

"It wouldn't hurt to ask; let me talk to somebody."

Bill stretched his weight against the car seat and let his breath out in a puff. He hit the steering wheel a couple of times with his fist and stared at the street.

"I talked to your old man. He's strictly against the idea."

"I don't care if he is," I settled back in the seat and crossed my legs. "I don't care what you do, I really don't. I've been thinking about quitting."

"You can't quit," Bill puffed. "They've got a lot of money tied up in you. In case you didn't know it, you're a big investment."

"Bill, I can quit any time I want to and nobody can stop me. You know that as well as I do. There's the Mann Act and a few other White Slavery laws that I've got over your head."

Once more, Bill let out his breath in a big puff. He shook his head the way a prize fighter does when he's been hit hard.

"What about John?" Bill drummed his fingers on the steering wheel, "He won't let you quit and you know it."

"I'm going to see about a divorce in the morning," I answered.

"Baby, you could get me killed," Bill said slowly. "I set you up for this deal and now you want to back down. Will you hustle for a couple of weeks until I can find another chippy?"

I stared out the windshield for a few minutes. It wouldn't be fair to Bill to put him on the spot, but I was thinking more about Tom. If I quit now and never told him, maybe he'd never find out. If he did, it would be too late. Because of Tom, I didn't want to go through with it, but there were other things to consider—the money, my convertible, nice clothes, and the other things that I could afford made me want to hustle.

Tom hadn't asked me to marry him, but I knew that he would, perhaps on our next date. I had fooled the men in the cafe, maybe I could go on fooling Tom. That thought made me feel cheap and rotten inside and somewhere along the line, I would have to tell him. Perhaps, he would forgive me if we were already married.

"I'll get you off the grease, but that's as far as I'll go," I said finally. "You start looking for another girl. Now, how about me talking to the guys?"

Bill gave a sigh of relief. His face held such a comical expression of relief that I wanted to laugh.

"I'll set things up and give you a call in a couple of days," Bill said. "But I'm not promising anything."

"There's nothing we can do at Grace's?" I asked. "Couldn't I stay with her until then?"

"She won't keep you and that's all there is to it," Bill shook his head. "We can't do a thing with her."

Bill drove me to the bus station and let me out. When I got home, John was sitting in the easy chair, reading the newspaper. He didn't even ask me why I was home. We were man and wife in name only and as far as I was concerned, we weren't even that. When I looked at him, I wondered why I had been so anxious to marry him and wished I had saved myself for Tom.

I waited all day Thursday for the phone to ring, but Bill never called me. That evening, I suggested to John that we drive over to Parkville and take in the strip shows. I wanted to hear the jokes that the comics were telling about me.

"Not me," John answered. "I don't want to be seen with you in that town."

"People won't recognize me and so what if they did," I answered angrily. My own husband was ashamed to be seen out in public with me. It made me sore. "If you don't want to come with me, I'll go alone."

"Wanda, I can't figure you out," John laid down his paper and gave me a steady look. "You can't seem to get to the bottom fast enough."

"Look who's talking—you should have thought of that before you put me in a whorehouse. I didn't even know there were such places until I married you!" I turned and glared at him, "I didn't want to become a prostitute, but you forced me to. Just remember that you made me hustle."

"Yes, I remember."

I didn't like the tone of his voice or the way he picked up his newspaper. I went into the bedroom and slammed the door. I threw myself across the bed and started crying. What did John want from me? I couldn't understand him. He had wanted me to hustle; he had begged, argued, coaxed, and had even slapped me around until I said yes. I was scared and reluctant when he took me to Blanche's. At first, I hadn't wanted to hustle and had been ashamed.

Now, I liked being a prostitute and I wanted to hustle. I discovered that there was a lot that a woman could like about this life. The money, the luxuries it could buy, and the way that many of the men treated me. Now, I had the chance to better myself and be in a better position than the other prostitutes. I felt that I'd be a sucker if I didn't take Bill's offer.

When I quit, that would be the time to be respectable. John came into the bedroom. He didn't say anything, but he changed his shirt and suit. I put on a very plain dress and a small amount of make up. We took John's car. I wanted to take my convertible, but John said no. I wanted to go so bad that I didn't argue with him.

We toured the night spots along the "strip" and I laughed louder than anyone when they told jokes about "Wanda the Whore." They weren't talking about me. They were talking about a girl who gave away a million dollars before she found out that it was worth a cent. The only reason Wanda charged ten dollars was to keep out the riff-raff. She would charge twenty, but it would keep out too many men.

They weren't talking about me. It was someone that I had created and wasn't really real. I felt Tom's influence over me and I was still the nice girl that he thought I was. That's how I felt when I listened to their jokes. I got a secret amusement out of the way that some of the jokes got under John's skin. One of the remarks that a comedian made was about Wanda's poor husband. It had a germ of truth in it that hit John square between the eyes.

On Friday, I sat beside the phone waiting for Bill to call. When John went out for some cigarettes, I called Tom long distance. He asked me for a date and I said O.K. We were to meet at six.

About five, I changed into the blue dress Tom liked so well. I had purchased a pair of eye glasses from the dime store. They were hardly more than window panes, but they helped to alter my appearance. I changed my hair a little and added some lipstick; no rouge, no mascara, just a touch of pale lipstick. When I looked myself over in the mirror, I thought sure that someone would have to look pretty close to recognize me.

"Where are you going?" John looked up from his cross word puzzle.

"Out," I snapped.

"Who is he?"

"Who's who?" I stopped in my tracks and turned to stare at him.

"The guy you're on the make for. It's pretty plain, everything you do gives you away," he answered quietly. "I've known for a couple of weeks that you've been cheating on me."

I stared at him. He was so smug, so sure of what he knew that I wanted to kill him.

"You've been spying on me, you dirty—" I called him every name that I could think of. John took it. He didn't want to, but he did.

"I can tell you one thing," he said, when I ran out of breath, "If he's a nice guy, you'll come back to me."

"What makes you think that?"

"No decent man will have you. You're the worst kind of a whore," John answered. "You're a whore at heart and you couldn't stay true to a man if you had to."

"I'll show you," I answered bitterly. I stormed out and slammed the door.

I hid my convertible in a garage in Parkville and met Tom at the bus station. As soon as he saw me, he grabbed me in his arms and kissed me. I explained that I had driven down with some friends. Tom took my arm and he was so excited over something that he led me up the street almost at a trot. I was gasping for breath when we reached the cafe. We took our back booth again. I couldn't think, I couldn't talk, all I could do was just look at him. He had a shy grin on his face and I knew he had something planned.

"I've got something for you," he said with that shy grin. In many ways, he was bashful, but I loved it. It was one of the things that made him so special. He took out a box and showed me the engagement ring inside. It took him a long time to clear his throat.

"Would you?"

That was all that he could say. His face turned red, he dropped his eyes and swallowed at the lump in his throat. I had planned to take my time in saying yes, but I couldn't hold myself or my eagerness back.

"Oh, it's beautiful," I said. "I'd love to."

I watched his strong hands as he took mine and slipped the ring on my finger. The diamond glittered in the light. I wanted to say something, to tell him how much I loved him, but I couldn't. Something held the words back and I couldn't.

"You know what it means?" he stammered, "How-when-when would you want to set the date?"

"Oh, Tom, I-I don't know. Don't you think—You don't know anything about me!"

"I don't need to know anything about you." He smiled at me. "I know all there is to know, I guess."

I shook my head. I wanted to tell him, but the words were locked up inside me. I didn't know how or where to begin. He didn't give me a chance, either.

"Let's go or we'll be late for the show," he said and grabbed my arm. "This is no time to start crying."

I brushed the tears from my eyes as we walked. It seemed that I was swimming, or this was some kind of dream, and a thousand thoughts crowded their way into my mind and tumbled over each other. I was happy, yet I needed to cry, and I knew I had plenty to cry about. I tried to imagine how Tom would feel towards me if I told him. If I knew that, it would make things easier.

In the movie, Tom slipped his arm around my shoulder. I scooted close and smiled up at him. I didn't want to leave this spot or for this moment to end. The sheltering darkness was so peaceful and wonderful. I leaned my head back so I could look at Tom's profile and I just thought about him. How nice he was, how I loved him, and how I would show my love for him after we were married.

Something happened to me and I didn't know what started it. Perhaps it was my thoughts about Tom or perhaps it was being so close to him, but when his hands touched me they sent fire racing through my body. I had never felt this way before and a funny kind of an excitement took hold of me. I wanted him and I couldn't control my feelings.

"Let's go," I whispered.

"Where to?"

He looked at me with surprise and turned his eyes towards the screen. He was interested in the show.

"Someplace—anywhere, I—I want to be alone with you," I whispered.

All that I could think about was how much I wanted him and I lost control of my emotions. I walked fast and led the way when we left the theater. Tom followed me, a puzzled look in his eyes. I stepped into the shadows of an alley.

"Kiss me, please," I begged.

Never had a kiss meant so much to me. When he lifted his lips from mine, I was so weak and light-headed that I could hardly stand up. I held onto his arms and rested my forehead against his chest. I gasped for breath when he started kissing me on my neck and ears. They sent little electric currents running through my body. I had done it plenty of times, but each time and with each man, I had always held something back. I didn't know what it was and there had been times that I tried not to hold back, to let go and enjoy myself. But even the few times with John, I had held myself in reserve. Now, for the first time in my life, I knew the meaning of the words passion and desire.

My entire body trembled from his kisses and tender love making. I couldn't tell him what I wanted, not in words, but I tried to tell him in kisses and actions, and to awaken in him the emotions that I felt. He was not experienced. If he had been, Tom would have realized sooner. I wondered if there had been any women in his life before me.

He led me down the street until we came to the high school stadium and Tom laid me down on one of the football bleachers. I looked up at the sky; a thousand stars pin-pointed its velvet. There was no moon and the stars stood out clear and bright. It's funny, I had never noticed the stars before this night.

I felt his kisses on my lips and felt his hands on my body. He held me close and started undressing me. I tried to help him, but I was all thumbs when I tried to unbutton my blouse. I had to let him do it.

In a moment, I was naked; my clothes tossed carelessly onto the ground and before him, I was ashamed of my nakedness. Sex had a different meaning to me; for the first time, a rightful meaning, and I knew that I could never give myself to another man. There were tears in my eyes because I was cheating Tom. For him, I should have been a virgin and at this hour, I knew what a woman's honor meant. I wanted to give it that, but my honor had been sold, and I prayed that he wouldn't care. I found out a lot of things in those few moments. I discovered the meaning of love. There is sex for pleasure and sex as an expression of love between two people, and the sex act for pleasure is as wrong as anything can be. I had met a man whom I loved and too late, I discovered what love and honor meant.

Tom sent joy surging through my body and made my nerves tingle. I tried to talk but I couldn't, and there were moments when I was afraid I would pass out. When his weight left my body, I was soaking wet with sweat. He stood there, looking down at me. It was too dark for me to see the expression on his face.

"Hold me, hold me!" I pleaded. I was afraid I would lose him.

He sat down and put my head on his knee. He held me close, his strong arms around me. I closed my eyes.

"I'm sorry," he whispered. "I guess we should have waited."

I shook my head and smiled up at him. I didn't want to talk, I just wanted him to hold me close.

"You'd better put your clothes on," he said. "I don't want you catching pneumonia."

I started dressing but only because he told me to. I didn't want to, I wanted to stay in his arms and stay naked before him. My clothes had been scattered over the ground and we had trouble finding them. I giggled like an embarrassed school girl. After I dressed, Tom sat down and had me put my head in his lap. We shared a cigarette, neither of us saying anything. We had already told each other of our love. There is a magic in silence, you can say so much by saying nothing.

He stamped the cigarette out, bent over, and kissed me.

"Darling, I love you. I can never love anyone the way I love you," he whispered.

"I feel the same way about you," I answered.

He scooted around so he could kiss me again. I giggled, not at anything, but just because I was happy.

"We'd better be going," he said. "It's time for my bus."

I didn't want to leave this spot or for Tom to leave me. I wished for a way to hold back the hours and I didn't want daylight to come.

The bus was there when we got to the bus station. We didn't have much time left. Tom held my hands in his, so he could look at the ring on my finger. I was conscious of the grass stains on my blouse and skirt. When I looked up into his eyes, I could see no questions about my honor or the men who had been to me before him. All I could see was complete happiness and no trace of doubt or questions. In a moment, he left me with a quick kiss.

I drove my convertible home, following the bus. If I couldn't be with him, I wanted to be as close to him as I possibly could. But my magic moments ended as soon as I reached home. John was in bed asleep, but he had left a note on the night stand for me. I was to call Bill in the morning. I wadded the note up and threw it away.

CHAPTER TWELVE

THE NEXT morning, I woke up excited and happy. I could hear John messing around in the kitchen. I sat up, put my arms around my knees and stared dreamily into space while I waited for him to bring me my breakfast. I was so happy that I wasn't even mad at John and in a way, I felt sorry for him. In a lot of ways, he had been pretty swell to me.

He had only been to me twice; that was during the first few weeks of our marriage. Since then, he had tried to have relations with me several times, but it had been no use. Ours was a sexless marriage, but John didn't seem to mind. He got a thrill, perhaps even a bigger thrill than the customer did, by watching me take on men. I had learned that men have a lot of ideas about what constitutes sexual enjoyment for them, and to please John, I let him hide in my room as often as I could.

In his own way, he loved me and John was different from other pimps. Most pimps play a girl strictly for her money and try to have several girls hustling for him, but John had never tried to get me a sister-in-law. One of the reasons he made me quit Blanche's was because she objected to his peeking and before he placed me in Grace's, he had made certain that she would let him watch.

When he brought the tray in and set it on the bed, I felt very close to John. I wanted to tell him about my night with Tom and how wonderful it had been, but I decided I'd better not. At least, not for awhile because John could get pretty jealous. In a way,

I felt it would be wrong to tell him because last night had been Tom's and my night. It would be wrong to share it with anyone.

John sat down on the bed and lit a cigarette. He stared down at the rug for a long time, then raised his eyes to look at me.

"Babe, I wish you wouldn't go through with it."

My heart gave a flip-flop. I had my mind on Tom and I wondered if John knew about us.

"You'll be getting in too deep," John continued. "I want you to quit one of these days and if you get mixed up with Bill and that bunch, you won't be able to."

John lapsed into silence. I guess he was waiting for my answer, but I didn't have one to give him. He laid his hand flat on the bed and stroked the covers with the palm of his hand.

"I did it because you wanted me to," I shrugged my shoulders. "Why don't you want me to go in with them—think of the money I'll make."

"You're a nice girl and I want to keep you that way."

"Aren't you a little late for that?" I felt a tiny twist of anger. "You should have thought of that a year ago."

"You think I didn't?" John looked at me with despair in his eyes. "I thought a lot about it—How do you think I've felt, watching you get ready every night to go to a whorehouse. I thought about it before we were married too. I thought I could start over again and things would be different with you."

His hand, rubbing across the cover, made a scratching noise. I knew that I should hate him, yet I felt sorry for him. I let my hand rest on his.

"What do you want me to do?"

"I don't know," John shook his head. "I didn't think very much about it until last night. I went to Parkville looking for you."

"You didn't find me, did you?" I gave a sigh of relief when he shook his head.

"But I was in a bar and I listened to a couple of men talk about you and the other girls on Green Street. It was pretty hard to take—hearing what they said about you and the names they called you," John kept his eyes to the floor. "I kept thinking—that's my wife they're talking about. I'm supposed to love and take care of her, but instead, look what I've done to her."

"Honey, I haven't complained, have I?" I asked and squeezed his hand. "I'm still the same girl, aren't I?"

"No, you haven't complained," John looked up at me and hesitated a moment. "If I asked you a question, will you give me an honest answer?"

"Yes."

"You've enjoyed being a prostitute, haven't you?"

I shrugged my shoulders. I didn't even know how to answer his question. I just hadn't thought about it, I guess. There had been moments when I could have answered yes and I had had moments when I had thought about killing myself. I suppose that I had enjoyed being a prostitute most of the time, but I couldn't tell him that. I just shrugged my shoulders again.

"I did it because you wanted me to," I answered. "You told me that if I didn't, you'd leave me, remember?"

John didn't answer. He just sat there with an odd twisted look on his face. I looked at him with pity.

"What do you want me to do?" I asked.

"I don't know—I don't know," John ground his cigarette into the ash tray and shook his head. "Do you suppose we could go someplace and start all over?"

"Where would we go?"

"I don't know—a long ways from here."

He looked at me and his look gave me a funny feeling. He was putting me on the spot. If we *could* start over, I wanted to go with him. Yet, there was Tom. I wanted Tom and I couldn't make up my mind which one I wanted the most. I loved Tom, but still I wanted to be with John. Before I could think out my answer, the phone rang. John sat motionless on the edge of the bed while I slipped on my robe and went into the living room to answer the phone. It was Bill.

"How come you haven't called?" he asked.

"I just woke up."

I started to tell him that I wasn't going through with it and that I wanted time to think things out, but Bill didn't give me a chance.

"Can you meet me in front of the Parkville Motel around one?" Bill asked.

He kept on talking and his voice sounded desperate as he pleaded with me. I turned around and saw John standing in the doorway.

"It's Bill. He says he has to talk to me. They've got a nice deal lined up for me."

"Where at? Under the high school bleachers?"

I watched John's face turn into a sneer and his words cut me like a whip. He had been spying on Tom and me. That's why he had wanted to get me out of town—to break us up. Sure, we'd start over—start over in another whorehouse. I glared across the room at John.

"Bill, I'll be right down," I hung up.

Angrily, I glared at John when I passed him. I went into our bedroom and started dressing. It hurt me to know that he had watched Tom and me. I hadn't minded it when he had watched me and my customers. But there had been something wonderful, something almost sacred about Tom's love making and John had desecrated it with his lust. He stood there, watching me.

"You're not quitting then?" he asked.

"Not your way, I'm not," I snapped. "You've said your pretty speech, now get out."

"I've known about you and that soldier for a long time," John said in an odd tone. "I just don't want to lose you."

"Get out!" I screamed and threw a cold cream jar at his head.

It missed him and I started crying. John stood there, watching me, but he didn't come near me. If he had, I would have scratched his eyes out.

"What are you going to do when he finds out you're nothing but a whore?"

There was no anger, no smirk in his voice. He said it so casually and so matter-of-fact that it made me even more angry.

"Nothing. He won't care."

"You'll find out different."

John slammed the door when he went out. I buried my face against my arm. I cried until there were no tears left inside me—just a dull, numb ache that wouldn't leave. I dried my eyes and finished dressing.

I burned up the highway to Parkview. I was so mad that I didn't care what Bill had set-up for me. As he had told me over the phone, I left my car a half block from the Motel and walked the rest of the way. My 'Bosses' were waiting in cabin 5. Bill opened the door a tiny crack and peeked out when I knocked.

"Hi, Wanda, come on in," he gave a nervous little laugh and licked his lips.

They had been putting the screws to him. Bill's collar was wet with sweat, his face red, and his hands were shaking. I wondered how such a guy ever got into the vice racket; he was too nice a guy to be pushing chippies around. He would have been a lot happier running a neighborhood grocery. He would have liked that, I thought, and he'd be the kind who would give candy to the kids because he liked them.

I went inside and Bill shut the door. He stood there, licking his lips, and trying to find something for his hands to do. Two men sitting at the table looked me over very closely. I pretended not to know them, but I did. I had seen their pictures in the Parkville paper several times. One was from the Mayor's office and the other was a detective on the vice squad. The one from the Mayor's office didn't mean that the Mayor was in on the take. The take had been going on long before the present Mayor had been elected and would go on after he was out of office.

"Sit down, Wanda," the man from the Mayor's office said.

His name was Jergens and the other man was Thomas. Jergens gave me a friendly smile and offered me a cigarette, but it was Thomas who held my interest. He was about forty, broad shouldered, with black wavy hair. I like the way he looked me over, straight faced, not a patronizing smile like Jergens. He'd be easy to talk business with, a lot easier than Jergens, because he'd regard it as strictly business. I felt he'd keep his word and wouldn't ditch me if there was trouble. Thomas finished looking me over and I wondered if he was pleased.

"Beat it," Thomas said to Bill.

Bill started to argue. He cleared his throat, but Thomas glared at him. Bill acted like a whipped pup. He went on out.

"What has Bill told you?" Jergens asked. I got that nervous little smile of his again.

"Nothing much—except that I'm to start hustling for you guys."

"Do you think you'll like that?"

"I don't know—I'm just a chippy, so it doesn't matter who I hustle for, I guess." I paused and shrugged my shoulders, "What's in it for me?"

"You ought to do as good as Margie has. Who knows, maybe better?"

"What do you want out of the deal?" Thomas asked.

"O.K., I'll lay it on the line. I'll hustle for you guys as long as you want me to. I won't kick or pull the shingles off of the roof when the men get tired of me and you bring in a new girl," I said. "But when I leave Green street, I want to leave with more than just the clothes on my back."

"What would you suggest?" Thomas asked.

"A better deal than you gave Margie," I answered. "Only instead of just me, I keep another girl and get a percentage of what she earns."

Jergens gave me a shocked look, but I think Thomas understood. I had two things to sell, an attractive body and my youth. I wouldn't have either very long and I have just a few years that I can be a prostitute. I knew how much I would probably earn on Green street and I figured that half what I took in should be mine—all clear.

I didn't want to barter or dicker over my body. I didn't want to think of my love as just a commodity to be sold, but for the moment I had to. Yet, I couldn't ask too much or they would say no. There are too many women who are willing to be prostitutes.

"Wanda, how old are you?" Thomas asked.

"Eighteen. But I've hustled for almost a year, so I know the ropes."

"Have you any money of your own to put into a house?" Jergens asked. He tapped a pencil on the table.

"No, you'll have to set me up and let me pay you back out of my share," I answered.

"We'll think it over," Jergens promised. He sounded a little doubtful.

"If we let you have a cat-house of your own, what kind of a joint will it be?" Thomas asked.

"Just another cat-house. I'll run it quiet and orderly," I promised.

"There's only one catch. A couple of preachers have been yelling about the red lights," Jergens said; he stretched his arms across the table and folded his hands. "The word from upstairs is to keep things quiet for awhile and I don't know if we can get by with opening another house. But we'll let you know."

I was dismissed just like that. I didn't get a chance to explain some things that I wanted to. I went outside into the bright sunlight and stood there a moment. Bill was sitting on the little stone wall that bordered the drive.

"What'd they say?" he asked, anxiously wiping his face with his handkerchief.

"Just that they'd let me know."

Bill tried to light a cigarette, but his hands were so sweaty that he had it soaking wet before he could light it. He threw it away with a disgusted motion.

"Is that all they asked you?"

"Just my age," I shrugged my shoulders, "I told them I was eighteen."

"You're going to get me killed yet," Bill said disgustedly. "I told them you were twenty-two."

"They'll probably believe you before they will me," I laughed.

We chatted for a few minutes and then I started home. Just as I entered our apartment, the phone started ringing. It was Bill.

"The boys say you could go to work for Mildred for a couple of days," Bill told me.

"What else did they say?" I asked.

"That's it." Bill hung up.

I packed all my things, even the pictures on the wall, and loaded them in my convertible. I was leaving John for good.

CHAPTER THIRTEEN

ILDRED WAS a short, plump woman about sixty and she was all sugar and spice when she met me at her door. She knew I had connections with the 'big boys' and she assumed that I was a girl friend of one of them. I didn't bother to tell her any different, but let her think whatever she pleased. She showed me every bedroom she had and told me to take my pick. I didn't want to dislodge any of her girls, so I took the vacant one.

I put what things and clothes that I would need in my room and locked the rest of my things in the trunk of my car. In a few minutes, I was ready for business. Mildred kept three girls, counting me, and whenever she introduced us to a customer, she made it a point to play me up.

I was somebody! I was Wanda. Her other girls looked at me with curious eyes and I wondered what they thought of me. I noticed that they made little or no attempts to get friendly with me. It was just like being at Grace's, except I didn't go home at night. My first night, I had thirty-three customers. Business was picking up.

The next morning, I hustled a couple of dates and then got ready to meet Tom. He was the big interest in my life and I went around dreaming about him. I was to meet him at two p.m. I kept myself in a daze just thinking about him. The way he looked at me, the things he had said, and the way he had kissed me, I kept reliving these things over in my mind.

The men who dated me didn't thrill me, and I didn't enjoy sex. As always, I only pretended. A successful prostitute is just an actress. I had learned the little gestures, the movements to make with my body, and to smile at the proper moments in order to make the customer believe I was enjoying our session. I guess men know that we don't enjoy relations with our customers, but each guy seems to think that he is the exception and that we can't help but like doing it with him. It would be pretty hard to convince a man that going to bed with him was as exciting as washing my face. If a chippy told that to a customer he would get mad, insult her, and make it out that it was her fault because she didn't.

A man can easily understand why a chippy doesn't enjoy it with all or some of her customers. He can understand that, but he can't understand why she doesn't enjoy it with *him*. Men are just not logical when it comes to sex.

So I got a smug satisfaction out of the little deceit that I played on the men. By nature, I am quiet and mousey. In high school, I was the leading wallflower, although this wasn't entirely my fault. My father's radical ideas about religion often caused me embarrassment and caused the other kids to stay away from me.

But dressed the way that I like to dress and walking naturally, I can pass customers on the street and not be recognized. In a cat-house, I am entirely different. I add make-up, fix my hair differently, and walk with a swing to my hips. There have been nights when my face actually ached from smiling so much. When a man walked through the door, I looked him over as closely as he did me. I tried to judge by his actions what kind of a girl he wanted and I tried to be like that girl. If he wanted a girl who was quiet and shy, I was shy and demure. If he wanted a girl who was red-hot and brassy, I could be that way too. Most of the time it was an easy ten bucks to earn, but occasionally, I had a guy treat me rough. But hustling is so easy, too easy if the truth is known.

If it was as bad as some of the people make it out to be, maybe there wouldn't be so many prostitutes.

I felt no shame in taking their money and I felt that I deserved it. I felt it was a fair bargain. He got the thrill he wanted from me, and he left me his mess to clean up. The fact that I didn't know the guy or anything about him made it easier for me to submit to him.

At Mildred's, I tried to live up to my reputation. I was a red-hot chippy who took on plenty of men and enjoyed them. It was silly what men believed about me. I was no different from the other girls on Green street, but my customers believed differently.

The vice syndicate that controlled Green street was strictly a home-made affair, owned and operated by local people. There was no head, no so-called vice lord who controlled everything, but a dozen or so people running the show. First, there were the girls. Most of them were married to or had pimps for boy friends. They hustled in the houses their guys put them in and didn't ask questions. To a prostitute, one whorehouse or one town is about the same as another.

I don't think anyone could ever untangle the graft that went on and discover to whom the money went. The people made money off of the houses in two ways, directly and indirectly. One was the graft and fines. That was the direct. The money the girls paid to Bill to get into the brothels. The pay-off to the vice cops who came around from time to time. The fines we paid each week and the health cards we had to buy.

Indirectly, was the rent. For example, a brothel on this street rented from five hundred to fifteen hundred dollars a month. The rent depended on the number of girls the Madame kept. The private residence along the block rented for from thirty to fifty dollars a month. The towel racket and the juke box concession were operated by two different groups. A jukebox was required in every brothel. Another indirect way is that chippys are notorious spenders and they spend every dime they make. The stores reaped a nice benefit.

On Green street, there are ten houses of prostitution, nine Madames, and sometimes as high as fifty prostitutes. Each girl charges a minimum of ten dollars a date and averages twenty dates a night. It figured out that the graft, rake-off, and fines that the chippies and Madames paid took about six dollars for each date a chippy had. Still no chippy could complain because most of the girls earned twenty to thirty thousand dollars a year.

Who got the loot from the houses? Its probably split up in so many different ways that it would be impossible to tell. Some of the brothels were owned and even financed by some of the city's leading business men. The house that Grace rented was owned by a lady in town who was famous for her charity works. At least some of her income came from prostitution. These people had invested in red light property the same way they invested in stocks and bonds. It was no secret that the Chief of Police bought a new car each year that cost more than his yearly salary.

But the men who gave the orders and controlled things didn't have any traffic with prostitutes. The only thing they cared about was that no local girls were found in the houses.

Jergens and Thomas were small fry who were investing money in me to set me up in business. They were in on the operation some way, but they received only crumbs. So they wanted more. The only way they could make more money was to put some girl in a whorehouse. Two of the girls on this street were secretly married to cops, but I guess the idea of being a pimp was distasteful to Jergens and Thomas. It amounted to the same thing, but they wanted to think of it as an investment. If the deal went through, it would be a sort of a partnership. They would stake me to a brothel of my own and instead of part of my earn-ings going to a Madame, it would go to them.

Bill was just a fall guy; hardly more than an errand boy. He collected the rent from the brothels, paid the girls' fines for them, and collected the rake-off. If something went wrong, he would take the rap, but it wasn't likely that anything would. The broth-els had been operating for over fifty years without a shut-down.

The next day, I went to the doctor for my examination, got my health card, and then went to the police station to give them my change of address and pay my next week's fine. The cops kid-ded me for awhile. I tried to find out if they had heard anything about my deal, but apparently they hadn't. When I left the sta-tion, it was time to meet Tom.

I forced myself to walk slow and take my time going to the bus station. I wanted him to have to wait for me, perhaps worry a little bit about me. It wouldn't be dark when our date would be over, so we wouldn't be able to go to the football field. As I walked down the hill, I paused to look into the store windows and won-dered what Tom would do about our love making. What I would do was more important. I wanted to give in to him, but I didn't want to appear cheap in his eyes.

Tom was waiting in front of the depot, smoking a cigarette, and pacing back and forth. I hurried the last half block and Tom walked towards me, a smile growing on his face. He caught me in his arms.

"I hurried as fast as I could," I laughed.

He held me a moment, looked at me, and I smiled up at him. The way he looked at me sent thrills running through me and no man had ever had that effect on me before.

"Are you hungry?"

"Starved," I answered.

He took my arm and we walked up the street to our little cafe. Tom was still smiling and talking to me, but I was too dizzy with joy to understand what he was saying. Just as we reached the cafe, I noticed some high school boys driving down the street in their hot rod.

"Hey, Wanda! How are things on Green street?" one of them yelled.

I froze, my hand on the door. Tom made a funny noise in his throat and turned around. They yelled something else and I heard them laugh. The way men do when they ridicule a prostitute in public.

"What in hell do you care?" a woman answered.

I looked around. There was another Wanda in town. She used to be on Green street, but now she was a drunk and part-time streetwalker. She was leaning against a lamp post in front of the cafe. I ducked into the cafe, Tom right behind me. I glanced over my shoulder at him; his face showed unconcern. I had been lucky. The boys had recognized me, but the other Wanda, standing there, had answered them. Through the window, I saw her stagger across the street, a cigarette dangling from her mouth, and she clutched a grimy white purse. She was so drunk she could hardly walk.

"Is she your Wanda too?" I smiled.

"Not hardly," Tom grinned and blushed like a school boy. "I just wish they would run those women out of town."

"Why?" I wrinkled up my nose at him.

"There's lot's of reasons," Tom answered bluntly and drummed his spoon against his coffee cup. "To begin with, a woman who is willing to lead that kind of life is mentally sick. Second, it's bad, bad for the town and everybody to have such places running wide open the way they do here. Look at those kids out there, still in high school, but they know about such women."

"Tom, what would you do if you found out I was one of those women?"

"You're not—you couldn't be." A touch of red rose to his face and I wondered if he thought he had betrayed me that night under the bleachers.

"But suppose I was?"

"I'm afraid our friendship would cease," Tom answered evenly. "I want a girl I can be proud of, not ashamed of. Do you think I'd want to marry a girl knowing that she'd done it with every Tom, Dick, and Harry? Or to have men make fun of her, the way those boys did that woman? No man in his right mind would want such a girl," Tom shook his head.

"Suppose you fell in love with a girl and then found out she was like that Wanda out there?"

"I'm afraid I'd fall out of love pretty fast," Tom laughed. He paused and gave me a somber look, "How come all the questions?"

I shrugged my shoulders and held my coffee cup before my face so it would hide my trembling lips.

"Can't I be curious about you?"

Tom gave me a pleased look. I didn't say anything more. I touched my face and my fingers were ice cold, yet they were sweating. I wanted to tell him. I tried to tell him, but if I had, he would have walked out on me for good. I couldn't stand that. He would find out or perhaps I would be able to tell him later on. But when he found out, maybe he would love me as much as I loved him and it wouldn't matter to him then. I wasn't being honest with him and I didn't like deceiving him, but I didn't know what else to do. I felt that it was better to deceive him and hold him to me than to be honest and lose him. I had promised to marry him, but I wouldn't until he learned the truth. I felt sure that I could make him understand when I did tell him. We ate dinner and left the cafe.

"Any place you want to go?" Tom asked. He gave me a cigarette and faced me to light it. I couldn't look him in the eye.

"The library," I answered. It was two blocks up the hill. We walked slowly, looking into all the windows.

"There's a suit I'd like to have," Tom said.

"Do you want me to buy it for you?" I asked. "I've got the money."

He gave me an odd look and shook his head. I guess he thought I was joking, but I wanted to buy him a suit or anything else that he wanted. I knew that I wouldn't feel so bad about being a prostitute if I could just give him the money I earned. At the library, he set down beside one of the marble lions that guarded the entrance.

"I want to finish my cigarette," he said. "I'll wait for you here."

I wanted him to come with me, but I said O. K. I hated being away from him for even a moment. I like to have something to read while I watch the streets for dates. It helps to pass away the time. The movie mags and the confessions that the other girls like, fail to interest me and I prefer poetry and the classics. I picked out a book of poems by Sara Teasdale and a book of I. S. Cobb's short stories. Next to Washington Irving, he is my favorite writer. I took them to the desk. The librarian gave me hard look as if she had seen me before and was trying to place me.

"Your name and address please," she said, stiff-lipped.

"Wanda Lane, 307 Green street."

Her eyes blazed with anger and she tore my card into little bits and flung the pieces into my face.

"You little harlot," she hissed. "Get out of here before I call the cops."

People in the library heard her shrill voice crack against the silence and looked up. I felt their eyes on me. I gasped and almost ran out of the library. Tom was coming up the steps. He turned and flung his cigarette into the street as I came through the door.

"What's the matter?"

"Nothing—nothing at all;" I was almost crying. "Come on, let's get out of here."

Tom hesitated, peering into the library. I went on down the steps, not waiting for him. I had to get him away from here, somehow. It kept ringing in my mind; I can't let him find out. It was a tiny prayer that I whispered. He came trailing after me and I slowed down when he caught up with me. I didn't look at him, but kept my head turned so he couldn't see my face.

"What happened?"

"Nothing."

"I didn't say—I mean, it's not me, is it?" he asked anxiously.

I shook my head. I was too choked up to try to talk.

"It's nothing I've done?"

"It's—It's—I made a phone call," I stammered. "I—I'll tell you later."

He walked beside me, quietly and not speaking, leaving me alone with my thoughts. I'd have to tell him something, but I didn't know what. Finally, I looked at him and managed to smile.

"That's better," Tom grinned.

"I'm O. K. now," I said.

We went to the matinee and it was a comedy. Tom held my hand and we both laughed through the picture. Whenever I looked at him, he'd squeeze my hand. I was in a bright mood when we left the show. We had about an hour until his bus left. We just walked up and down the street, holding hands. When we came to the hotel, Tom stopped; his face told me what he was thinking.

"Would—would you want to—to—" Tom started blushing.

I wanted to. But I didn't want to look cheap in his eyes and I was afraid I would if I said yes. Maybe I wouldn't now, but afterwards—He thought I was a nice girl and I wanted him to keep on believing that. He took my arm and started for the door. I stopped and pulled my arm away. He turned and looked at me.

"No, Boy, you're not pulling anything like that," I said.

"I should have known better," he gave me a foolish grin, "You're not mad, are you? You can't blame a guy for trying."

"Of course not," I answered. "I couldn't get mad at you for anything."

"You say that now," he grinned. "But after we're married, I bet you'll find plenty to get mad about."

We had coffee in the cafe and at the station, he kissed me good-by twice before the bus got there.

"How about Friday night?" he suggested.

Friday would be pay night and the Madame would be sore at me if I wasn't on the turf that night.

"Sunday," I promised.

He kissed me again and he was the last one on the bus. Before the bus was out of sight, I was the loneliest woman in the world.

CHAPTER FOURTEEN

WHEN I GOT back to Mildred's, Bill was waiting out in front for me. I got into his car and we started driving. He would cut up one street and down another to make sure that we weren't being followed.

"Heard from your old man lately?" Bill asked.

"Not since I ditched him. He's probably got another girl on the string by now. He'd have to, or else give up eating."

Bill didn't crack a smile. We were zipping along the highway. Bill squinted into the rear view mirror. The highway behind us was pitch dark. He turned off onto a dirt sideroad.

"You don't think he'll cause us any trouble, do you? The boys have got a lot of money tied in this deal. They've mortgaged their homes and have borrowed all they could just to set you up in business."

"How much do they think it's going to cost?"

"Sixty thousand, at least. The boys who pull the strings aren't too interested in having another whorehouse, so they've upped the price," Bill answered. "There's been a lot of pressure put on city hall to close down Green street."

Sixty thousand bucks. I was to pay half. I was over thirty thousand dollars in debt already. It would take me almost three years to pay off that sixty thousand. It would be three years, maybe more, before Jergens, Thomas, or I would make any money off of the deal.

Bill stopped the car. We were on a lonely sideroad and we could see down the road a mile each way. Bill leaned back in the seat and pulled out a pack of cigarettes. He offered me one and I waited until he tapped the end of his own on the steering wheel for him to light it for me.

"They've got a joint located for you—309 Green," Bill said. He handed me a key. It was to a locker. "Take this to the bus station tomorrow morning. You'll find the sixty grand there. I guess you know what to do with it?"

"Yeah, I know."

"The boys said to tell you that sixty grand is a lot of money, and for you or that husband of yours not to get any funny ideas," Bill said. "They plan to protect their investment. In plain words, don't try to skip—you won't make it."

"You make it sound like a spy movie or something," I laughed.

"Babe, it's no laughing matter. I'm just sorry that I'm mixed up in it," Bill said slowly. "If you were smart, you'd get out now. They ain't doing this because they like you, you know that. They figure on getting every dime back and they won't care what you have to do to get it for them."

I was silent. Bill slowly beat his hand against the steering wheel.

"You're too young to understand, I guess," Bill continued, "but I've known a lot of nice girls like you. They were nice when they started out, but before they were through, they were as hard as nails. Why don't you get out now while you've got the chance?"

"Bill, I don't like sermons," I said. I didn't like him talking to me this way. It gave me a funny feeling inside.

"I just don't want to see you end up in the gutter the way so many girls do."

"Well, you'd better be taking me back," I snapped. "I'm wasting a lot of valuable time."

Bill shot me an angry glance. He wanted to say more, but I wasn't in any mood to listen. He rolled his shoulders and started the motor. It was about eight when we reached Mildred's. I got out of the car without another word.

"There's been a lot of men asking for you," Mildred said when I walked in.

"I'm sorry, but I had business with Bill."

I went on upstairs to my room and changed my clothes. I could hear the girl in the next room laughing with a customer and I wished I had something to laugh about. Bill's words had got under my skin.

That night was like so many others that I had spent on Green street. I took a man's money, went to bed with him, and five minutes after he was gone, I had forgotten what he had said and his face. Business was starting to pick up along Green street. Often, when I finished hustling a date, I would find men waiting in the parlor for a girl. The other houses were just as busy and men don't like to be kept waiting. The Madames would soon be adding girls to their staffs.

I could hardly wait until I got my own place started. As the deal was now, by the time I divided with Jergens, the Madame, and paid my graft, I was hustling for my room and board.

At ten, the next morning, my alarm started blasting in my ear. It was a struggle to force myself out of bed. My back ached from hustling so many dates. I dressed and drove to the bus station. I looked around but saw no one that I knew. If anyone was following me, either I didn't know them or they were out of sight. I didn't care, but I was curious. I opened the locker and took out the packet. I knew what to do with the money, Bill had wised me up on that point. As I started to leave, I nearly flopped with surprise. There stood John!

I hardly recognized him; his eyes were blood shot with drink and his lean face was even more pinched. He stood before me, his clothes wrinkled and dirty, and weaving in his tracks.

"Wanda—Wanda, I want to talk to you," his voice was almost a whine.

When I shook my head, he spread his hands out to me.

"Look, Honey, can't—can't we pick up where we left off. I—I need you," he pleaded.

"It's over—all over."

I started to go around him, but he grabbed my arms. When he did that, a man stepped down from the shoe shine stand and started towards us. He stopped between the benches and waited. I drew back the packet and gripped it tight. I didn't want John to get that. The anger rose in his eyes.

"I heard you've become an uptown whore with high powered connections and everything. You think those guys will take care of you the way I did?"

"I'll take care of myself," I snapped. "Now, get out of my way or I'll call a cop."

John dropped his hands in despair. He looked at me and there was something terrible in his expression; his face was that of a dead man's.

"I—I can't live without you—I love you so much," he whispered. "I—I didn't know it until you walked out on me. I—I'm no good—I know that—but I'm worse without you. We—we'll do things your way—you won't have to hustle or be a prostitute any more."

He was starting to raise his voice and people were beginning to look at us. Hastily, I started digging into my pocket book. I had to get rid of him before trouble started. I had almost a hundred dollars in my coin purse and I wadded the bills into his hands.

"Here, don't bother me again," I said.

He clutched the money and I darted around him. John didn't try to follow me. He just stood there; staring at the money. I got into my convertible and roared off; nearly hitting a taxi when I pulled out into the street. I made my first stop a corner pay phone and called Thomas.

"Hey, that old man of mine is liable to cause trouble," I said. I was afraid that he might go to Tom and tell him about me. "He's liable to pull the shingles off the roof."

"I heard about the deal in the bus station," Thomas answered casually. "Don't worry, we'll take care of things, and see that he let's you alone."

"I got a hot love affair going with a guy and I don't want John spoiling it," I said. "Can you make sure that he don't?"

"I think so," Thomas answered casually.

He seemed so indifferent that it worried me. When I hung up the phone, I was scared. I was scared for myself, scared that Tom would find out, and I was scared for John. I remembered the different warnings that John had put out about joining up with Jergens and Thomas. I knew I couldn't expect any mercy from them, I wasn't expecting any, but hustling for John, I could argue with him. I could say no once in awhile. I wouldn't be able to do that now.

This would be a good chance to quit, but I knew that I wouldn't take it. I didn't want to quit and I felt I could hustle, escape the pitfalls, and come out ahead. My first stop was the police station.

The Chief of Police was in conference and I had to cool my heels in the corridor for over an hour. Thomas walked past me several times, but we didn't even look at each other. It seemed ages before I was ushered into the Chief's office. Smith was about sixty, with snow white hair, and a ruddy complexion. He leaned back in his chair and hung one arm over the back when I went in.

"Well, Wanda, what can I do for you?" he asked. He motioned for me to take the chair beside his desk.

"I guess you know that I am an inmate of a house of prostitution on Green street?" I said. I didn't know how much he knew, so I played it straight to begin with. He smiled at my formal statement.

"I'm aware of that," his eyes narrowed with expectation.

"Well, I've got a chance to improve my situation and I would like your permission to start another brothel and keep another girl besides myself," I said.

He frowned and tapped his desk with a pencil.

"Aren't you a little young to be thinking about becoming a Madame? I would much rather see you quit the life you're leading."

"I have no intention of becoming a Madame," I answered. "If I'm going to hustle, I might as well be hustling for myself."

"Wanda, I don't want to see a young girl like you tying herself down to red light property. If you do that, you'll be ruining your chances of ever quitting," Smith said slowly. "If I had my way, I'd close all those houses, but I don't have my way. Now, there's a business club that I am active in and one of our main projects is the rehabilitation of prostitutes from Green street. So far this year, we have helped five women return to a decent life. If you want me to, I'll turn your name in to the club. You'll receive the best medical and psychiatric care, and a job."

I shook my head. Smith paused and leaned back in his chair.

"Why don't you think about it for a couple of days? I'll have a couple of girls who we have helped talk to you," Brown argued, "I'm sure if you talk to them, you'll give our plan a try. You're a very unusual woman, Wanda, and I don't want to see you run the route to skid row."

"I'm no different from the other girls," I answered. "I just take the trouble to add."

Smith chuckled. "I have a complaint from the librarian here in town. Seems you tried to borrow some books from the library. That's a little unusual for a prostitute. If you would spend the energy in some other field that you are in prostitution, you could make a success of yourself. That's why I want to help you."

I shook my head, wadded up an envelope, and threw it into the waste basket. He didn't pay any attention to it and I wondered if he knew there was forty thousand dollars in it. If he did, he didn't seem to care.

"It's no use. I'm in so deep now that I'll never get out," I said. "I'll just promise you that I'll run an orderly place of business and try not to cause any trouble."

Smith shrugged his shoulders.

"I can't stop you from being a prostitute, but I wish you would think over my offer." He hesitated. "No matter how things look on the surface, it's an honest deal."

"I'm sure that it is and someday I may take you up on it," I answered and walked out.

My next stop was the Sheriff's office and I wondered what part he played in it. There were so many fingers in the pie, it was hard to tell who was who. They had cut Green street up into so many pieces that there was no telling. When I entered the Sheriff's office, he was busy writing. He was about thirty-five, and looked like an ex-football player with his big shoulders. He hardly looked up at me. I made my little speech and waited. He kept on writing.

"There's the waste basket," he said.

His pen didn't miss a stroke. I tossed the envelope with twenty grand into it and walked out. I didn't care too much for the way he had treated me. A guy who felt that way could cause trouble.

As I returned to Mildred's, I did some thinking. It was going to cost about seventy thousand dollars in graft just to open another brothel on Green street and Jergens and Thomas didn't have that kind of money, so who was backing them? Maybe the guy was backing them the same way they were backing me. You don't just hang a red light on the front porch and run a want ad for prostitutes. There are too many state and federal laws involved. Someone has to take the risk and run the joint. If something went wrong, I would take the rap. If they traced it to Jergens and Thomas, say a grand jury or something, they couldn't trace it any further. They might take a fall, but the guys who were really behind it wouldn't be touched. If something happened to me, they could easily get another prostitute.

I drove past 309. It was a pretty trashy looking place. A family with three small kids lived there and almost every Saturday night, the cops had to arrest the old man for beating up on his wife. The rent had been jumped from twenty-five dollars to five hundred a month.

The family in 309 moved out late that afternoon and early the next morning, Bill was by after me. We walked down to take a look at the inside. It was pretty shabby on the outside, some of the weather boarding had rotted at the ends and other pieces had been split off. The kids had scribbled with crayons all over the front. The window screens were torn and rusty. The supports beneath the porch were so rotten that I was afraid we would fall through.

Bill unlocked the front door and with a flourish gave me the key. It was a bent skeleton key and a kid could have opened the latch with an ice pick. I had expected it to be dirty, but I didn't think they would leave it half as bad as they did. There were piles of trash in the corners and the woodwork was black with dirt. What wallpaper remained had been written on by the kids and there were gaps in the plaster.

"Good Lord," Bill said. He touched the ceiling with his hand and the whole thing almost came down on our heads.

I went on through the house. Despite its run-down condition, it wasn't too bad and it could be fixed up. The way the house had been built and the rooms arranged, it was well suited for a cat-house. The parlor was in front and on the other side were two bedrooms. The bath was located between them. Through the living room archway was a small dining room and on back was the kitchen. The way the doors were arranged, the men could have as much privacy as they could expect. Any one going down the street, could only see into the parlor. It would cost plenty to fix it up, but the people who owned it had agreed to pay half.

"I want a gas floor furnace here," I said to Bill, motioning towards the arch way. "And I want a gas heater in each bedroom. I want a wash basin in each bed room and separate hot water heaters for each one."

"Two water heaters?"

"Three—one for the kitchen." I saw his funny look and laughed. "Honey, hot water is a must in this business."

Bill sighed and scribbled in his note book.

"Can't we do something with the outside? That porch is a mess," I added. "Some drunk might fall through and break his neck."

"I'll take care of the floors and walls too," he added. "Anything else?"

"New doors and locks—good strong locks."

I returned to Mildred's. She wasn't too happy about a new whorehouse starting up and she complained about it. There was too much competition along the street already and a new brothel would just take business from the other houses. I knew the other Madames felt the same way and they were doing plenty of squawking.

From her window, I could see the workmen come and go. There were so many of them that I wondered how they managed to keep out of each others' way. The outside was covered with bright green shingles and a cute little concrete stoop was poured. While Bill was at it, he had the house rewired and new fixtures took the place of the ugly drop cords. I forced myself to stay away even though I was so anxious that I could hardly wait. I hardly paid any attention to the men coming down the street and Mildred had to remind me severel times to motion to them. I was too engrossed in watching the workmen. Bill came by that evening with a progress report.

He went on down to Margie's and told her to leave. She was crying when Bill loaded her suitcases into his car and drove off with her. A girl from Annie's moved in just as soon as Bill was out of sight. Kathy and her husband made an awfully nice couple and they took over. Kathy was about twenty-three, with light brown hair, and I guess the nicest pair of legs on Green street. Margie's had been just a three room house. Kathy set in the front room, with her legs propped up and her dress pulled back, so the men on the sidewalk could see her legs. Through the window, I could see her husband sitting in the kitchen playing solitaire.

Two afternoons later, Bill drove up and motioned for me. I ran out to his car.

This time, there was a little stoop and a new walk leading up to it; nice shiny window screens and a brand new door. Bill slipped the key into the latch and opened it. I held my breath when I went in. There were even new hardwood floors and they had fixed everything the way I had wanted them to. I had the same thrill now that I'd had when I was ten and my mother surprised me with a doll for Christmas. I wanted to take this house into my arms and love it the way I had loved that doll.

"Oh Bill, it's heavenly!" I cried. I threw my arms around his neck and started kissing him without even thinking. He just chuckled and patted me on the fanny.

"Will you come with me?" I pleaded.

Together, we toured every paint shop in town. I was so excited that I didn't know which colors and designs to pick out. There were so many that I couldn't make up my mind.

"Why don't you call an interior decorator and let him do it?" Bill suggested.

"No, I want to do this myself," I answered. I wanted to do something with my hands, to work on something.

"Jeez, you act like you're going to live there the rest of your life," he grumbled.

His words hurt. They stung and the sting went deep. I had forgotten that it was to be just another brothel.

"I'm sorry," Bill mumbled.

"It's O. K. I needed to be reminded."

After that, I didn't have any trouble picking out the paint and paper. I selected a light shade of blue for the bedrooms because I have always thought blue was a romantic color. The living room paper was flowered.

"Will you help me paper it? I know how," I told Bill. "I used to help my mother at home."

"How do I get into these messes?" Bill sighed and shook his head. "You'd better get someone else to do it; you're time is pretty valuable."

I let Bill take care of the details and went on to buy my furniture. When I returned to Mildred's, Bill called and said my place of business would be ready in two days.

When the men were through, I loaded my stuff into my car and moved in. I had brought sheets, pillow cases, even dishes, and I was looking forward to cooking. It was so heavenly, that I didn't want to leave it for a minute. It was mine, but if Bill said the word, I would be out in five minutes and another girl in. I had no real security, but the furniture was mine and for once, I owned more than just the clothes on my back. That was the important thing. The first to visit me was the laundry man. He left eight dozen towels.

"That's 96 towels," I said, "What do you think I am, anyway?"

"Oh, I know what you are," he grinned. "I don't want you to run out. Maybe I ought to leave you another dozen."

He brought in another bundle and I paid him. About ten, Bill showed up and a truck from a sign company pulled up right behind him. I stared at the neon sign that they lifted out of the truck. The letters were over a foot tall and read WANDA LANE.

"I—I don't want that—that thing," I almost screamed at Bill. The men stood there, awkwardly holding it. Bill took a step back.

"What's the matter with it?"

"It—It's a—a Madame sign," I broke into tears. "I—I don't want people to think I'm a Madame."

Bill chuckled and led me into the house. He motioned for the men to hang the sign in the north picture window.

"You're a long ways from that—nobody is going to think you're a Madame," he sat down in an easy chair and held my hand. "The boys just want to make sure the guys find you. When you've got a product to sell, you advertise it."

I tried to dry my eyes. There was nothing I could say or do. The sign was in and I watched the men test it.

"Leave it on," Bill told them and looked at me. "You want to go out and look at it?"

"No," I cut him off short.

Bill stood up and glanced around the room. He twirled his hat in his hand and gave me a pat on the shoulder.

"The boys have decided that you don't need a Madame—not for awhile anyway," he said, "The hustler they're sending you can do that part for you. Her name's Rosie—she's a nice kid. You'll like her."

I didn't answer. I just stared down at the floor. Bill paused in the doorway, making awkward motions with his hands while he waited for me to answer. When he saw that I wasn't going to, he went on out. I didn't like being pushed or feel that I was nothing more than a brand of cigarettes or something or to be advertised.

The door bell rang and there stood a delivery boy with two bunches of roses. He set them on the table and hurried out like he was embarrassed. Both cards read: "Good luck from the boys." I wanted to cry again. It was the first time that anyone had ever sent me flowers. Even Grace sent me a dozen for my 'opening' and the ones from the Chief of Police arrived late that evening.

A taxi pulled up and I gave a groan when Rosie got out. She was about forty and she had a back end that looked a mile wide. She had a nice face, but that was about all, and no guy would go for a dame that old. She planted her suitcases in the living room.

"I'm Rosie," she said with a little laugh, "I guess you're going to keep me?"

"Not me, sister, you should have retired ten years ago," I snapped. "Just as soon as I can get hold of Bill, you're gone."

"Wait, Honey, you don't know about me," she pleaded. "Maybe I ain't so young, but I still can earn plenty of money."

I was on the phone, trying to get Bill, but he didn't answer.

"Here, let me show you something," she said breathlessly. She took off her blouse and slipped down her slip. "See?"

She turned around so I could see her back. It was a lace work of white scars.

"I'm an exhibition gal," Rosie said. "I've got a string of steady customers who pay plenty to work me over."

"What do they use on you—barb wire?" I asked. She took me seriously.

"No one has ever used that, but just about everything else. I'll let them use any kind of a whip they want to. Let me show you."

She opened one of her suitcases. It was filled with chains, straps, pieces of ropes, whips, switches, and paddles of all kinds and description. She took out an aluminum switch and giggled when she twirled it. It made a humming noise in the air that sent chills up and down my spine.

"All I can say is that you earn your bucks the hard way."

"It's easier than straight dates and I enjoy it as much as they do," she answered. "Wait until you've hustled as long as I have; you'll turn to something for your kicks."

I knew there were plenty of men who liked to torture women and I had already met my share of them. I had met the perverts who like to spank women or be spanked by them. I had let them use a strap or paddle on my fanny several times, but I didn't enjoy it. It was an ordeal that I had to grit my teeth to bear. But to let them use a whip or to draw blood—I couldn't imagine any woman being willing to go that far.

"Stick around," I said. I was curious to see if she was telling the truth.

"I'll earn you plenty," she promised. I showed her her bedroom. "Gosh, it's pretty. It's sure nice being in a whorehouse again. You don't know how awful it is not to be. I'd rather be a street light on Green street than the richest dame on Gold Coast."

She hung her clothes in the closet and I watched her put her instruments away with loving care. The man came with the rabbit hutches and pigeon coops and I showed him where to set them up in the back yard. I asked Rosie if she would like to take care of them and she said yes. I didn't want to see them, knowing what would happen to them. I went back to the parlor. My sign was still on. I thought about turning it off, but I didn't. I didn't feel like getting up and turning off the switch.

CHAPTER FIFTEEN

WHILE ROSIE was out taking care of the animals, I hooked my first customer. I got a real thrill out of escorting him into my bedroom. Before, I had looked upon cat-house bedrooms in about the same way that I had bus station or filling station rest rooms. It was for my use, but it wasn't personally mine and I was conscious of the fact that countless other chippies had used the room before I did. They had left their scratches, cigarette burns on the dresser, and other marks. When a mattress wore out, the Madame brought a new one. When the men got tired of a chippy, the Madame ordered another one in about the same way she ordered the mattress.

But this bedroom was different. It was my own personal bedroom. It showed my tastes, my ideas of beauty, and if a room can, some of my own personality. It made my engagement with my customer seem more real and intimate. After he left me, I wondered if I would feel that way towards all my customers and I hoped I would. I didn't want this place to become just another whorehouse and I didn't want to be just another whore. I wanted to be something special to the men who came to me.

I hooked three dates that afternoon. I really tried to show them a good time and pretend I enjoyed it. I told them to come back again.

It's funny, being a whore. I don't think anything about it when a man turns up my walk or asks me how much I charge. It doesn't bother me to take his money or to undress before him.

The look of admiration in their eyes when I strip, the eager way they come to me makes prostitution seem O.K. I feel that I've known the guy all my life and it's right and proper for us to do it. Somehow, I can believe that I am his and I belong to him. Perhaps, I feel the same way that a wife feels towards her husband after they've been married a long time, I don't know.

But when it's over and I watch the customer put on his clothes, it gives me a funny feeling to know that he's going to walk out on me the same casual way that he walked into my bedroom. It gives me a feeling of regret and uselessness to know that I mean nothing to him.

A man uses a prostitute for his own pleasure, only a prostitute can never see it that way. It gives my conscience a jolt to see a guy who has been to me several times turn into another whorehouse. Sometimes, when I'm alone, I'll suddenly remember the face of some customer. Perhaps he only came to me just one time and I've never seen him since. I don't know his name or anything about him. But for the moment, I wonder about him and if he remembers me.

A prostitute gives more than just her body to a man, she gives up a tiny drop of her soul. I may be just merchandise to a Madame or some vice ring, but I can't look upon my own body that way. I pay for the money I earn and I don't earn it as easy as people think I do.

When it got dark, the men started coming. It's always that way on a red light street. The men wait until it's dark because they are ashamed they'll be recognized. The men waited in the semi-dark living room that was between the kitchen and the parlor. Just as soon as one got through, I would slip on my panties and peek into the living room. If no one was there, I would slip on my pajama bottoms, go into the parlor to flop in the easy chair beside the window, and light a cigarette. But I didn't get very many chances to try out my easy chair as there were generally men waiting in the living room. Once, there were six guys waiting for me.

"Next," I'd say, and hold the door open. I would smile up at him and try to show pleasure with my eyes.

"Sorry to keep you waiting, but they've really been giving me a work out," I would say. "Now, how would you like to have it?"

It gave most of the guys a thrill when I told them I was getting a work out. Since all I had to do was kick off my panties, I could lay down and catch my breath while he undressed. It was restful, just to stare up at the ceiling for a moment's peace. When he started to get into bed, I would look at him and smile again.

If he tried to kiss me, I would turn my face and take his kiss on my cheek. It's screwy, I know, but all prostitutes have nutty ideas. I couldn't let a man kiss me. I felt that my kisses were only for Tom and someday the rest of me would be his alone too.

"You come back and see me, Honey, maybe the next time I won't be so busy and you can stay longer," I would say before I opened the door.

I smiled so much that there were moments that I felt my face would crack like it was made out of plaster. My insides were sore and swollen from so many dates and some of the men hurt me so much that I had to grit my teeth from the pain. The muscles in my back ached from so much twisting.

Each time I ushered in a new customer, there was that twinge of fear that this one would discover that I was a phoney, and that my sexual enjoyment was only a pretense and a game that I was playing for their benefit. But none of them seemed to notice and so many of them were so childish in their eagerness to get in bed with me that they reminded me of naked little boys. Perhaps the most amusing part is the guys who pause to ask me how or why I'm a prostitute.

"I guess I'm lucky," was my stock answer. The men like it and it's an answer they are willing to believe.

So far, I've never had a man to ask me that before he got into bed with me. That question always comes while they are pulling on their pants. If they would ask me that at the door, they might have their answer. When a guy is so shook up over going to bed with me that I have to help him unzip his pants, I know why I'm a chippy. Most men aren't very particular about whom they have relations with, and most of the time, all they think about is their own pleasure. They can get the urge so bad or strong that they are glad to pay a woman. As long as men want it that bad, they'll hunt until they find a woman who is willing to sell. They'll always be prostitutes.

Prostitution, even our moral code concerning sex, is all in the man's favor and is a pretty one-sided affair. I've checked a lot of books out of the library about prostitution. Some of them have been pretty truthful and accurate and others were so far from reality that it was pitiful. Some of the books, especially by doctors and social workers, claim that prostitutes and their customers are emotionally ill. If my customers are emotionally ill, there are sure a lot of nuts running loose. I think that nature made the sex drive in men so he would go out seeking women. It's just a man's normal nature to go hunting for a woman and have relations with her without any love or strings attached. A damn man can cheat on his wife and go home to her without a flicker of conscience. Men have made it a national sport to brag about their conquests, even if their conquest is only a whore like me.

But all the books seem to fail in pointing out one thing. As soon as one prostitute leaves this racket, another one takes her place. That the demand for prostitutes never ends, and men will flock to a dame who puts out for cash. My own opinion is that prostitution is the natural result of a man's normal sex drive.

It gives a man a feeling of superiority to lay a woman and he thinks he is dominating her. I know because I've watched a lot of them leave my body and how they acted and what they've said. They can think they 'own' me in the same way they own their wives and they can forget the men waiting in the living room for me.

I'm not saying that prostitution should be legalized and looked upon as an honorable profession. I think that would be just as wrong as it is to hound us, treat us like criminals, and make us outcasts.

Somewhere in between is the answer. I have no idea where. Perhaps I am emotionally sick, I don't know. Perhaps, if I had married the right guy, I wouldn't have wound up on Green street. But if I had married the right guy, I might have ended up taking on every man in the neighborhood. There are wives who cheat constantly on their husbands, just as there are plenty of wives who hate to have sex relations and give their husband ten bucks and send him to me. That happens all the time.

By the way prostitution is set up in this country now, the men get the fun, and everyone but the prostitute gets her money.

I took on fifty-seven men my opening night and I was dog tired when I quit. Rosie was real swell to me. She changed the sheet on my bed and fixed my supper. Afterwards, she gave me a rub down to take the kinks out of my back. Already the foot board of my bed had been scratched and scuffed by men who hadn't bothered to take off their shoes. I even had one guy who started to get in bed with his hat on and he got sore when I made him take it off.

Fifty-seven men for me and ten for Rosie. I lay there in bed and just relaxed, feeling Rosie's gentle hands stroking my back.

I was pleased with myself and I knew the boys would be happy. I stayed awake while Rosie pinned up my hair, but I felt myself slide off into comfortable cozy blackness of sleep when she rubbed cold cream on my face.

CHAPTER SIXTEEN

ROSIE WOKE me about ten. She had already cleaned up the house. After I had my coffee, she gave me a manicure, combed out my hair and fixed it. We had forgotten to buy groceries, so I dressed and drove to the store while she got my room ready for business. When I returned, she was on the phone calling her customers, and telling them her new address. She laughed, giggled, and talked about ten minutes to each one.

I stretched out in the chair beside the window and started watching the street for dates. Rosie placed a footstool beneath my feet. It was the damn waiting that I despised. I read every item in the newspaper and tossed it over to Rosie. The only thing that interested me was the coming election and I wondered if it would have any effect on Green street.

The laundry man came with his load of towels and usual good humor, and the knock at the back door meant that the guy that Joe sent around wanted his daily ten. A couple of boys from the vice squad came around and proudly, I showed off my house to them. They even stopped to have a cup of coffee with me and we sat in the kitchen and talked. They teased me about being so popular and I slipped them twenty bucks. They sneaked out the back door when we heard a customer come in the front. The customer had come at the wrong time. If he had waited a few minutes, the cops might have gone to bed with me and I could have hustled their take.

I wasn't too glad to see the customer anyway. He was a real slob and I had done business with him before. Rosie took him out in back to help him select a pigeon. I heard Rosie give him a sales pitch for herself and I kept hoping he would buy her. She could put out for him a lot better than I could. I hated to have my room messed up.

I put a huge piece of oil cloth over the bed and I was naked and lying down when they returned. I didn't smile at him and I put my elbow over my eyes so I wouldn't see the pigeon. Poor little creature! It makes me sad to look at them before it happens and see the look in their eyes.

I could hear his harsh breathing and the chair scrape on the floor while he undressed. His body was wet with sweat, yet clammy, when he touched my skin and his breath was rank in my face. I turned my face towards the wall and tried to keep my mind blank while I met the movements of his body. It's hard not to think, but I have a trick that I use. I play solitaire with an imaginary deck of cards. It takes effort to concentrate and keep the plays straight in my mind.

He stopped. I gritted my teeth and clamped my eyes shut. I heard the pigeon squawk when he twisted its head off. I heard him laugh, chuckling to himself in a weird way that made the chills run up my back, when he held the bird up so the blood would spurt over my body.

The slob! The slob, I thought. Why can't he love me the way a man is supposed to?

It was over. I was covered with blood that started sticking to my skin. When I looked at the guy, excitement danced in his eyes. He started talking about it, making elated gestures with his hands while he talked. The act had been like drink to him. I managed to get rid of him and I slid into the tub of hot water that Rosie had drawn for me.

"That dirty son of a bitch," I said. "I hate a slob like that!"

Rosie was in my room, cleaning up the mess. I felt better after calling him those names.

"You've never done it just for the pleasure of doing it, have you?" Rosie asked.

"Course I have—what makes you think I haven't?" I snapped. I thought of that time at the high school with Tom.

"No, you haven't. I don't think you could love anybody but yourself," Rosie answered. "You think of sex as something to use to get what you want. If you ever loved a man, you'd know that sex and violence are mixed together."

"What do you know about it? Hell, you're nothing but a flagger," I snapped. "Sure, for you, they're mixed. You get your kicks from a whip."

"I haven't always been. You don't know how to give yourself completely to a man—to have him bite and kiss your body."

"Monkey bites, I know. I've had 'em."

Rosie shook her head. "Honey, you still don't understand. I mean to love just an ordinary guy and when he's through making love to you, you're so weak that you couldn't think about doing it with another man. Love is something to give, not to sell, and the bedroom is only a small part of it. It's the part that counts least when you're in love."

"You're nuts. Hell—all a man wants from a woman is sex. That's all he cares about."

"That's where you're wrong, child," Rosie answered. "You don't know how wrong you are."

"I'm no child. I'm eighteen years old and I know plenty about men!" I almost yelled at her. "I don't want anyone preaching at me. I had enough of that when I was home."

"Nobody is preaching to you," she said. "But what are you going to do in a few years when you've got a big butt and lines in your face? You'll find out that there's more to being a woman than just getting screwed. It's funny. When you're young and pretty, you take the customers for granted and when you get older and could really show them a good time because you really want to, they turn you down. Maybe you don't think so much about it now, but someday you will."

"I said I don't want any sermons," I said bitterly. "I know about men, all of them, and I know what they want from women."

Even Tom, who wanted to marry me, had been on the make for me. He had tried to pull me into a hotel for a session.

"O.K. no more sermons," Rosie laughed.

I drained the tub. Rosie scrubbed it out, filled it again, and I got in once more. I lay submerged to my neck while she cleaned up my room and washed off the oil cloth. I wondered if we could afford to hire a maid to take care of such things.

My body was clean, but I still felt dirty and grimy when I got out of the tub. It would be awhile before that feeling would wear off. My room was all clean and there were no marks to show that the slob had been there. I noted with satisfaction that he hadn't got blood on the wall paper. I couldn't bring myself to dress. I wanted to be naked until the feeling that I had wore off. I put on a pair of slippers and roamed the house like a nervous animal. The blinds were drawn and no one could see in, but I didn't care if people did see me naked.

"You'd better take care of business," Rosie suggested.

I frowned at her, put on my clothes and took my place at the window. It was a lonesome and useless wait. About four, the boy threw the evening paper on the porch and I read it through. On one of the back pages, I saw where John Lane had been arrested for violation of the Mann Act. It had happened three states and five hundred miles from here. I called Thomas and told him about it. He didn't seem too concerned, but said he would look into it and call me back.

All I could do was wait.

When it started to get-dark, Rosie turned on my light and it drew men the way it drew bugs. About five-thirty, Bill picked me up and we drove out to a lonely country road. Thomas drove up behind us. I got into his car and he started driving.

He told me about John. My husband had pulled about as dumb a trick that a pimp could pull. Somewhere, he had picked up two teen-age sisters, the oldest was sixteen, and had put them in a house of prostitution. The girls' parents had him arrested.

"How bad is it?" I asked.

"Pretty bad," Thomas answered. "He must have been drunk or else he wanted to get caught."

The last remained in my mind. Maybe he was trying to get even with me or perhaps he wanted to hurt himself. He had been too smart to pull a deal like that.

"This isn't a frame, is it?" I glanced at Thomas. "You said you were going to get rid of him."

"No, it's no frame," Thomas answered. "We got rid of him. I bought him a ticket to St. Louis and told him to use it."

Thomas looked at me and hesitated; "Does he mean anything to you?"

"Not any more—but I feel responsible for him. Do you know what I mean?"

"Well, don't. He ain't worth it," Thomas growled. He parked the car beneath a tree and looked at me, "Who's your boy friend now?"

"Nobody," I answered. "There's no one now."

I leaned my head back against the seat. Thomas was looking at me, as if he was trying to make up his mind. When he did, he leaned forward and kissed me. I didn't move.

"I've been waiting for you to do that," I said.

"Why?"

"I don't know—I've just been wanting you to," I shrugged my shoulders.

"I can't figure you dames out—as many times a day that—"

"Don't try to figure us out," I interrupted. "Don't say anything—just let me pretend there hasn't been anyone else."

He took me in his arms. I tried to imagine he was the only one and that I wasn't a prostitute. I relaxed beneath his kisses and tried to return his passion, but that part wasn't in me. The only thing I gained from it was that I no longer felt so self-conscious in front of him now and I felt sure I could get what I wanted from him. I kept thinking about what Rosie had said—about me just using sex to get what I wanted. I didn't want to be that way.

Thomas gave me John's lawyer's name and let me out again where Bill was parked. Bill took me back to Green street.

I thought about going to see John, but I couldn't leave here very well, and the truth was that I didn't want to see him. It was over between us and I didn't want to have it start over. But I did call John's lawyer and had a long talk with him. He told me that John's chances were black and suggested that I stay out of it because it might go harder on John if the judge knew that his wife was a chippy. I promised to send him some money and hung up.

I started to go to bed but Bill and Jergens showed up to collect their share of my earnings. There was no chance to cheat them. They knew exactly how many men I had done business with. What we had to go over was my expenses and the money I had spent.

"What's this twenty bucks a day to Joe?" Bill asked.

"You ought to know about that," I answered. "Every gal on this street pays off to him—ten bucks a day."

Bill and Jergens exchanged glances.

"What gives?" I asked. "What's wrong?"

"I don't know, but we'll find out." Bill gave me a worried frown.

They left and in hour, Thomas stopped by and asked me about the pay off to Joe. I told him what I had told Bill and Jergens.

"Who do you think it is?" I asked.

"I don't know—it might be some mob from St. Louis or Chicago trying to move in," Thomas said. "You haven't heard of any girls hustling him?"

I shook my head.

"You didn't ask questions?"

"No, everybody was scared to, I guess," I answered. "We just gave him ten bucks and kept our mouths shut."

Thomas shook his head again. "See you tomorrow," he said.

CHAPTER SEVENTEEN

A COUPLE OF HOURS after Thomas left, I was awakened by someone hammering on the back door and heard Rosie grumbling as she went to see who it was. A vague thought came into my mind that this was Saturday and it would be a rough night on little Wanda. But tomorrow was Sunday and I would have a date with Tom. The hammering stopped and I went back to sleep. I heard men's voices as I dozed off, but I didn't know or care who it was.

Rosie woke me about noon. She had taken care of the laundry man, phoned the drug store to send over what we needed, ordered some groceries, and had taken care of the numerous little items that needed to be done. I liked the way she handled things and I was beginning to like her.

"Who was here?" I stretched and yawned.

"Jergens and Bill—they're still here," Rosie answered. "They want to talk to this guy who's been making a drag for Joe. Honey, I don't like it—why do they have to pick our joint?"

"I don't know." I slipped out of bed and put on my robe. They were sitting in the kitchen drinking whiskey from some water glasses.

"What goes? I don't want trouble, what's the idea of picking my joint?" I asked.

"We won't make you any trouble," Bill promised.

"You won't, but what about this Joe? I'm on the other side of the fence, you know," I said. "I'd rather pay the ten bucks than risk getting into trouble."

"Maybe you would, but we want to find out who is trying to move in," Bill answered.

I didn't get a chance to argue. The guy knocked on the back door and I recognized his knock. I froze in my tracks. Bill and Jergens moved out of sight and motioned for me to open the door. I could feel the goose pimples on my legs scratch against my robe and my legs were like wooden pins, so stiff they would hardly take me to the door. I pulled it open.

"Joe sent me—he wants ten bucks apiece from you girls," the man said.

"Come on in," I said and moved back out of the way.

When he stepped through the door, Bill slammed it shut and they both grabbed him. He didn't have much of a chance and he let out a whine and stopped fighting when Bill twisted his arm behind his back.

"Frisk him," Bill ordered. Rosie ran her hands over his clothes. She came up with a notebook and a bundle of tens and twenties. They slammed him into a chair. The guy caught a deep breath.

"You cops?" he asked and shrugged his shoulders.

"Tell us about it," Bill said. "Who's Joe and what goes?"

The guy gave a weak little smile. He hunched his shoulders and smiled again at them.

"I'm Joe," he said in a timid voice. "Pretty good racket, wasn't it? I just told them that Joe wanted ten and all these whores gave me ten bucks. They didn't ask questions, they just gave it to me."

Again, he gave a weak little laugh. Bill just stared at him with a disgusted look on his face. He went into the front room and made a phone call. He looked a little pale when he returned.

"What would you have done if a dame had said no?" Bill asked.

"There's nothing I could have done," Joe smiled at Bill.

"Where did you get the bright idea for this shake down?" Bill's neck turned red with anger. The man shrugged his shoulders. I felt sorry for him and he reminded me of a homeless pup.

"The mills were shut down and I was out of work," he began, "I—I saw you cops taking money from these women and I thought that I could do the same thing. It wouldn't be any worse for me to take some of their money than it is for a cop. So I went up to one of the houses and told the lady that Joe wanted ten bucks from every girl. The old gal paid off and didn't say a word, so I went to the next house. That's how it happened."

"You formed an awful bad habit," Bill muttered. He took the man by his arm, "Come on. Let's go."

Joe gave us his weak little smile and went with them. I laid down and slept until about three. I was still groggy with sleep, but I fixed my hair and make-up. Rosie helped me select an outfit that we thought the men would like. I felt pretty nervous and jittery when I took my place at the window. Too many things were happening to me and I couldn't keep up with them.

That night was about the hardest that I ever spent on the turf. The men went hard with me and it seemed that each customer said or did something that irritated me. They hurt me more than usual. But each moment brought me closer to my date with Tom and I worried about having to tell him before he found out some other way. It had only been luck that he hadn't discovered it so far. But how does a woman explain to a guy like Tom that she's a whore? I knew what he thought of the women on Green street.

It was past three-thirty in the morning before we turned out the lights. Once more, Rosie went through the ritual of taking care of me, putting up my hair, cleansing my body, and giving me a rub down.

"Make me look real pretty," I whispered to her. "I'm meeting a special guy tomorrow. By the way, when are all those high paying customers going to come around and see you?"

Rosie just laughed. I didn't care if she was lying or not. I liked the way she mothered and took care of me. She took on an occasional date and she was earning her room and board. Thomas hadn't been so dumb when he sent her to me. I was glad he did. I went to sleep while she was giving me a rub down.

Sunday morning, I didn't sleep in. It was too big a day in my life and I woke up early. I was so nervous and excited about meeting Tom that I couldn't hold onto anything. My hands weren't shaking or anything, but it just seemed that everything just flew out of my hands. I dropped almost everything I picked up.

"No customers for me this morning," I told Rosie.

I called Lois. Whenever a Madame got caught short and needed a girl for a night or two, they called her. She wasn't interested in hustling full time, but she liked the extra money once in awhile. She was married to a truck driver and they had a nice home and two kids in another city. Lois said she'd hustle for me today.

I had more than a hundred dresses in my closet and it took me over an hour to pick out one that I thought would be suitable to wear for my date with Tom. I wanted one that would really show off my figure, but I didn't want anything that would suggest that I was a strumpet. John had selected most of my dresses to wear on the turf and so many of them were cut too low in front to wear out on the street. I finally picked one that was full in front, but open enough to give him a shy peek if he stood close to me.

I added a pale lipstick to my lips and an even lighter shade of rouge to my cheeks. When I finished, I surveyed myself in my full length mirror for over fifteen minutes to make sure that everything was perfect. I called in Rosie.

"Tell me, do I look like a whore?" I turned around so she could see me.

"Honey, you look wonderful," Rosie said.

The thought of looking like a whore scared me. I had heard men say they could tell a prostitute just by looking at them. I didn't know if they could or not, but I didn't want anyone to tell it today. Rosie made some final touches with a comb to my hair and gave me a playful slap on the fanny with her hand.

"Go on and have a good time," she laughed.

When I stepped into the inner living room, I stopped in surprise. There was a man sitting on the sofa. He had taken off his shirt and shoes and was stretched out, reading a newspaper. He was black headed, about thirty-five, and had a puffed out belly that hung flabbily over his belt. He was a pimp, a lousy fancy man. His clothes, his perfume, and his soft white hands told me all I needed to know about him. My first thought was that he was Rosie's man.

"Who are you?" I asked.

"Tony," he gave me a grin that was almost a sneer. "Say, you're better looking than I thought you would be."

"Is he your guy?" I turned to Rosie. She shook her head. Tony laid his paper down and fished into his coat for a cigarette.

"No, starting now, I'm your guy," he smiled up at me. "I heard you ain't got a pimp any more. Your husband is going to be away for awhile, so I thought I'd look after his interests. A nice little chippy like you needs a guy to look after her."

"Like Hell," I blazed. I went into the parlor and called Thomas.

"Get over here as fast as you—"

That's as far as I got. Tony grabbed the phone out of my hands and slapped me. I stumbled and fell against the sofa. He grabbed my dress, jerked me up, slapped me again, then shoved me to the floor. He stood over me, his hands on his hips.

"Listen, Babe, you're hustling for me so you might as well get used to it," he said and picked up my pocket book. I had five hundred dollars saved up to send to John's lawyer. Tony counted it and shoved it into his pocket. "You're doing O.K. Wanda, I can see that we're going to get along swell."

In the distance, I heard the siren on Thomas's squad car. He cut it before he turned the corner. He pulled up in front of the house and came in on the run.

"What's the trouble?" he stormed.

"This damn pimp is trying to move in on me," I sobbed. My cheeks stung from his slaps, but I didn't start crying until Thomas came through the door.

"Beat it," Thomas snarled.

Tony glared at Thomas for a moment, then shrugged his shoulders indifferently. He sat down and started putting on his shirt.

"I heard she was on the loose," Tony mumbled.

"She is," Thomas answered.

"Then what the hell?" Tony raised his face to Thomas. "What do you care if she keeps a guy or not. A damn whore ain't got no business with money. What do you expect her to do with it— stick it in the bank for her old age?"

Thomas didn't answer. Tony bent over and laced up his shoes.

"Maybe she's your girl," Tony looked up at Thomas. "Maybe she is," he shrugged his shoulders. "Man, I never thought you'd turn pimp!"

Thomas' face turned black with fury. Tony threw up his hands to protect his face when Thomas bounded across the room. Thomas hit him once. Tony was sitting down, but he didn't get up. He just sat there, blood spurting from his lips. Thomas backed away, clinching and unclinching his fists. Tony didn't say anything. He just put on his coat.

"My money," I cried.

Tony tossed my roll onto the floor and walked out. He didn't slam the door, but shut it gently. He went down the steps, holding a handkerchief to his lips.

"He called me a pimp," Thomas shook with rage. He looked at me and his eyes widened, "I—I guess I am one. All my life, I've hated those rats, now—now I'm one myself."

"No, you're not," I said. "You didn't put me on the turf, you've helped me. It's just a business deal, that's all."

He stared at me for a moment and then went out; his face had a grim look when he drove off. I waited until he left then I hurried to meet Tom. At the telegraph office, I sent the money to John's lawyer, and almost ran to the bus station. Tom had brought his car.

After dinner in our little cafe, we went to the zoo. We spent the afternoon looking at the animals and Tom had brought a blanket for me to lie on. I laid on my stomach and watched the sun make its westward journey. Tom sat beside me, one leg propped under him.

"I love you," I whispered.

I kept my face turned from him because I didn't want him to see my tears. I was so happy that I was crying. I felt that way when I was with him. I realized how weak and ineffective our language is to convey emotion. Three little words couldn't begin to tell him how I felt. He put his hand on my back.

It sent fire racing through me and even the nerves in my feet tingled. Before now, I had never believed that a man could have this much effect on me. I wanted to move myself beneath his hand, but there were people walking up and down the sidewalk.

"Tom, there's no one but you," I turned and looked at him. I had it on the tip of my tongue to tell him, but I couldn't. Everything was perfect and I was afraid I would destroy my happiness.

"Let's go," he said.

"Where?"

"Oh, just someplace," Tom smiled.

Tom folded the blanket and we drove far out into the country, through narrow country lanes that twisted through the hills until we came to a lonely spot that overlooked the river. The view was so beautiful that it took my breath away. The river looked like a silver strand woven into a green cloth and the hills in the distance; on the other side of the plain were a thousand hues of blue and purple.

Tom drew me close to him, and let his hand slip into my dress. I laid my head against his shoulder and looked out at the river. He squeezed gently.

"Don't rush me, Tony, let me think about it," I whispered.

"Tony!"

Tom stiffened and gave me a shocked look. It took me a moment to realize who's name I had said. Tony, the pimp who had tried to move in on me. I laughed to cover up and wondered why I had said his name.

"Tom—can't a girl have more than one boy friend?" I smiled up at him.

"Sounds like he runs a push cart," Tom growled. He frowned down at me.

"You're jealous," I teased, but it pleased me.

"You darn right I am. I don't want my girl playing the field. Now who's Tony?"

"A name I made up, to see what you'd say."

Tom grinned. He believed me. He kissed me, and I felt the strength of his hands when he gripped me and searched beneath my dress for my sensitive spots. He could build a fire inside me and it frightened me the way he could control me.

In almost a frenzy, I tore off my dress and slip. Tom had never seen me naked, not in the daylight anyway, and more than anything, I wanted to show myself completely to him. It was important that he see every bit of me. His hands were clumsy as he tried to help me. I laughed when I tossed my clothes into the back seat and I sat motionless while Tom looked at me. The look in his eyes and the expression on his face made me dizzy. I felt him kissing me and I tried to help him. Something wonderful had come over me and it seemed that I was a robot, unable to refuse his commands. When he laid me down on the car seat, I tried to pretend that I wasn't experienced.

When he was through with me, I dressed quickly. I wasn't ashamed of my nakedness, but with his eagerness gone, he would feel self-conscious. I leaned back in the seat, so exhausted that I could hardly move. Neither of us had much to say on the way back to Parkville. There wasn't much we could say, our love had been expressed in motion and action; words weren't needed now.

We took in a movie. Tom sat close to me and he would lean over, squeeze my hand and whisper, "Darling, I love you."

His car made complications, but I didn't think of it until we got out of the show.

"I'll drive you home," Tom said.

I fought for breath and his words made me panic. I felt as if someone had suddenly thrown cold water on me.

"No—no," I said quickly.

"Why not?" Tom turned and looked at me, "You never have showed me where you live. I don't even know the address. For all I know, you could be married."

Perhaps it was the look in my eyes or the way I moved my hands. I don't know. But he came closer to me, an odd look on his face that frightened me.

"Is—is that it, you're married?" his voice was stern.

"No—no!" I shook my head. I was frantic. I was trying to think of something to tell him, but my mind was blank, "Please, Tom, be reasonable."

"I am being reasonable," he said, "I think you ought to tell me where you live."

We were standing in a dark doorway and Tom had pressed against the window. Suddenly, he grabbed my purse and started rummaging through my purse. I saw the look of horror in his eyes when he read aloud my driver's license.

"Mrs. Wanda Lane, 309 Green street—Mrs.—then you're married!"

I sank back against the window, my teeth chattering.

"Yes—yes, I'm married, but—but we're not together. I—I've filed for a divorce," That much was the truth. When I had wired the money to John's lawyer, I had told him I wanted a divorce. "We—we parted before I met you."

I heard his breath slide out and I wondered if he was angry. I looked into his face, but I couldn't tell how he felt.

"Why didn't you tell me this?"

"I—I was afraid to—afraid I'd lose you," I stammered. "That's why I didn't want you coming around the house until after the divorce. Don't you understand?"

I gripped his arms. Tom just looked at me.

"All right, we'll do it your way," he answered. "Where can I let you off?"

"Here—this is as good a place as any."

He took me into his arms and held me close. I tried to show my love for him in our kiss.

"I'll see you Wednesday night," he said. "Same time, same place."

"I'll be there," I promised.

He turned and walked away. I watched him leave me. I loved the cut of his shoulders, the way he talked, and the way he looked at me when he whispered "I love you." Tom waved when he drove past. Everything was O.K. I was sure nothing could kill our love! I went back to the joint. Lois was sitting in the window when I got there.

"You didn't miss anything—it's been a dull night," she said when I walked in. "I didn't even get a good work-out."

"Maybe Wednesday will be better for you," I said. "I can use you then."

"O.K." Lois smiled as if she was pleased. I helped her gather up her things. She had brought her youngest baby with her, a cute little year-old boy. He had been asleep in the kitchen and he barely stirred when she picked him up.

"Cute," I said.

"Cute, but a nuisance," Lois answered and kissed him on the cheek. "I wish I could find someone to take care of him for awhile—I'd hustle full time—until we got our place paid for."

She slipped out the back door and I heard her drive off. I changed into something more suitable and took my chair in the parlor. Rosie was sprawled out on the sofa, drinking a can of beer.

"I won't be with you tomorrow night—I'm going to a party," she said. "Don't worry, I'll earn more there than you will in two nights on this street."

I waited a couple of hours, but no one came to me. It was as if the men had suddenly forgot where the houses were or that we were waiting for them. In disgust, I snapped out the light and went to bed.

CHAPTER EIGHTEEN

OLD BLUE MONDAY lived up to its name. The clouds, soggy with rain, hung low overhead and the gray smoke from the mills swirled at my feet when I stepped outside to get the milk and newspapers. I read through them fast, but saw nothing about John. Then I read the headline on the front page.

Joe, the little man who had run his shakedown racket, had been found in the river. He had gone for a swim without taking off his cement overshoes. I remembered how he had smiled at me when they had taken him away, and it gave me the shakes. We had paid off because we were scared, but someone in this town was more scared than we could ever hope to be and I wondered who had done the job.

Thomas? No, not he, he wouldn't take that kind of risk. Bill and Jergens? Perhaps, but more likely Joe had been turned over to a couple of pimps and maybe he had known more than he had let on. According to the paper, it had been a gangland killing, but they had failed to establish any connection between him and any mobsters. Perhaps he had been a witness to some crime, the paper suggested.

I sent Rosie over to the police station to pay our fines, and I settled back in my chair to hustle dates. This was becoming a sixteen to eighteen hour grind and the monotony was beginning to get me. It had been a lot different hustling for a Madame. Here, I had to hustle every date that I possibly could in order to stay in business. Actually, I was earning a lot less than I had when I

hustled for Grace. But I didn't have a Madame nagging me all the time and once I had things paid for, I would be O.K.

Bill came around to collect before Rosie got back. I could see that he had been in on the killing. For once, he didn't joke and his jowls shook with fright. I felt sorry for him. Bill wasn't the kind who could go around with a killing on his mind and he had a look in his eyes that made me think that he would soon crack.

"How are things going?" I asked at the door.

"They've gone too far this time—we'll never get away with it," he mumbled. "I told them we—we shouldn't—"

He caught himself and went on out. I had the funny feeling that I would never see him again.

For some reason, Monday morning brought me a steady stream of customers. I wasn't rushed nor did any of them have to wait for me, but for the rest of the morning and the early part of the afternoon, I was making two and three trips an hour to my bedroom. I like hustling when I'm not rushed and I don't have to hurry my customers. I judge whether I like a guy or not by his hands on my body. Some are rough and try to hurt me, but others were gentle with me.

I don't know where the trade was coming from nor who the guys were; most of them had never been to me before. The only one I recognized was a guy from the box factory. He had been a steady of mine ever since I came to Green Street.

"You know I'd like to take you home and raise you as a pet," he said while we were sitting on the bed talking. It made me smile at him.

"I'm afraid I'd be an awful expensive pet," I answered.

"Oh, I'd let you keep working," he grinned.

His words pleased me and made me feel good. He didn't care if I was a prostitute and maybe Tom wouldn't either. I thought about Lois. She was living the way I hoped Tom and I would live after we were married. Her husband was a square guy and he wasn't a pimp. He had a good job, but he wasn't making enough to buy the things they needed or wanted. They had talked it over and Lois and he had decided that it wouldn't hurt for her to do a little hustling.

She had a nice home in the suburbs of a city near here and as far as her neighbors were concerned, she was just a house-wife and a mother, and they didn't know about her little jaunts to Parkville.

Maybe Tom would let me hustle that way for awhile.

About three, I stepped outside to get a breath of fresh air and to watch for the paper boy. Beverly, one of the girls who hustled next door, was standing in the narrow space between the houses. She was smoking a cigarette and was naked beneath her house coat. She was about thirty-five, perhaps older. Once Rosie had commented that Beverly was one of the two whores that Noah put on his ark. There were lines of bitterness around her mouth and sadness lay deep in her eyes. Beverly looked at me and smiled, and we said "hi" to each other.

"You didn't go for Tony? He's a nice guy," she said.

When I shook my head, she looked at me with her funny little smile.

"Are you Tony's girl?" I asked.

"One of Tony's girls," she corrected. "I have two sister-in-laws. That's the only way for women like us to live. Sure, it's rough to share the guy you love with other women, but it's nice to have sister-in-laws too. You've got someone to talk to and who speaks the same language you do—like a family. Tony's a real swell guy—you'd like him."

"No thanks," I shook my head. The paper boy tossed me my paper and he looked surprised when I caught it.

There was nothing about John, but there was a piece about Bill. In a narrow alley uptown, he had been killed by a hit-and-run driver. The driver had escaped in the fog. Joe wasn't even mentioned. The paper said that Bill was a salesman for a typewriter concern and there was mention of his vice connections.

Rosie was primping to go to her party and she was as excited as a girl on her first date. About six, a car pulled up for her and Rosie just laughed when I told her to have a nice time. Monday night was one of the busiest nights that I ever had on Green street and it was seldom that there weren't men waiting in the parlor for me. The fact that they had to wait only seemed to make them more excited. I soon lost count of the number of dates that I had, but when I locked up for the night, I had almost seven hundred dollars. It was almost daylight.

I never did hear Rosie come in. But when I woke up the next morning, I could hear her humming in the kitchen as she fixed breakfast.

"Very hungry?" she asked.

"I could eat a horse," I answered.

She turned, gave me such an odd look that it puzzled me, then gave a funny little laugh. She was pleased with herself, I could tell. While we drank our coffee, she laid a thousand dollars on the table.

"This is what I earned last night," she said. "I told you I would bring in the money."

"Yeah, but what does your back look like—hamburger?" I took five hundred and put it in my bra.

"I've got a few marks, not many." She gave her head a toss. "That thousand came pretty easy, easier than your money does. You ought to give it a try."

I gave it a thought. A thousand bucks. I couldn't earn that much on Green street in one night. It wasn't possible.

"I'm willing," I said after a moment. "They can't do anything to me that hasn't been done before. If they can, I want to see it."

"They'll show you," Rosie's eyes danced with a secret grin. She laughed and almost ran to the phone. In a moment, she returned. "There's one set for tonight. You're on the bill."

Today might not be too bad, but there was a wrestling match tonight at the auditorium and it would keep trade away from Green street. Something like that always does. Rosie told me the Madame's name was Little Bits and she ran a house in Marshal. I had never heard of her.

Little Bits picked me up about six. She was barely five foot tall, with jet black hair and eyes, and a real slender body. She was about twenty-five and already a Madame. She had three girls with her.

The girl sitting with Little Bits in the front seat was a prostitute that I guessed to be about twenty-five or six. I sat in the rear, between the other two. One was about my age, a tall blonde. The other one was a brunette and she couldn't have been more than fourteen or fifteen. She was so excited that I suspected she was on dope.

"Have you ever been to a sex exhibition before?" Dorothy, the teen-ager, asked me.

"No, have you?"

"Plenty," she answered and she didn't sound like she was bragging.

She told me that she was in high school at Marshal and that she wasn't a chippy.

"Oh, I take a man on once in a while for dough," she admitted, "but not for no lousy five bucks a throw the way you girls do. That's for the birds."

"Honey, it's easier to find ten men with five bucks apiece than it is one man with fifty," the tall blonde cut in.

"All I want is a few kicks, I'm not interested in the dough," Dorothy answered.

The tall blonde, Mabel, gave me the set-up. Little Bits ran a five dollar house in Marshal, but we were going to a private brothel that she ran on the side. It was so exclusive that the patrons were carefully screened before they were admitted and admission to the party was a thousand bucks.

"The people we cater to can afford it," Mabel explained.

We turned off onto a dirt road and then onto another side road and finally stopped before a high wire gate. The brothel was a lonely farm house way out in the country and far off the road. It was surrounded by high barb wire fence and no one was allowed inside unless they had an invitation.

Cars were thick in the parking lot and I saw almost as many women as I did men entering the house. There was a large dining room and living room downstairs. Upstairs, there were six bedrooms. We were early and Little Bits showed us through the house and the equipment in the bedrooms. She laid out paddles, chains, leather straps, and other instruments of torture.

"I'll see that they don't mark you or cut you up any," Little Bits promised. "But you might as well expect to get several good butt blisterings before you get out of here."

She gave a funny little laugh. We went downstairs to the dining room. The party started off with a banquet and there were over thirty people seated at the table that was in the shape of a horseshoe. Almost half of the guests were women. I glanced around the table. I could see queers and lesbians quietly making love and I could smell the rope-like odor of marijuana cigarettes. I took a sip of wine and it gave me a wonderful giddy feeling.

The lady next to me was about forty, well upholstered, and her fingers and wrists were loaded with diamonds. I couldn't keep my eyes off of them. She smiled at me and started rubbing my knees with her hand. I couldn't have stopped her if I had wanted to. The place had got hold of me and I felt like I was in a dream.

Two Lesbians and two Homos did a comedy act while we were being served. It was funny to some of the guests and it was suggestive more than it was lewd. I glanced around the table and recognized many of the guests from their photos in the society pages.

The "Queer" act caused the guests to loosen up and they began to call for "Little Bits" and they applauded when she stood up. She smiled and stripped off her clothes. Her flesh wasn't soft and flabby the way most women's is, but it looked to be all muscles and as hard as nails.

She picked up cards off the table and money tossed onto the floor without using her hands. Her face was flushed with pleasure when she returned to her chair.

The next to perform was Dorothy, the little teen-ager. She lay down on a table in the center and I almost screamed when they brought a shetland pony in to her. Dorothy balanced herself on the table. She kept her face turned towards us and it seemed that she was staring at me. She had a smile on her face, but the smile was a mask, and I could see the pain in her eyes.

This place wasn't real. It didn't exist. It was a nightmare being shared by thirty people at the same time. You lose your fears and inhibitions in a dream and that was what these people were doing. The world and the people outside have a standard that they live by and they expect others to live by it too. They have a thousand rules of conduct and morals for us to obey.

But these people have their own rules too. Outside, they live the way they are required to, but when they came here, they took another set of laws. The laws that the outside world forbids. Here, the abnormal became the normal and degeneration was an accepted form of behavior. Torture and pain became a sexual thrill to receive and to give.

I downed my wine and it hit me. The room swam before my eyes and when I grasped my throat and stood up, I heard them laughing at me. I had been drugged with an aphrodisiac. Someone tore my clothes off of me and I think I helped them. I knew what I was doing, partly what I was saying, but I couldn't control myself. They dragged me to the wall and chained my hands above my head. I yelled and screamed and tried to free myself, but the chains only bit deeper into my hands. Suddenly, everything went black and I could no longer hear their laughter.

When I came to, most of the guests were upstairs. Occasionally, some man or women would come by, turn my chains so I faced the wall, and would take a paddle to my fanny. It gave them pleasure to see me laugh and scream and try to get away from the lashes. Yet, I didn't actually feel the pain. At least, not the way I was used to feeling pain. In a crazy way, the pain and the sting of the whips delighted me, and I looked upon the whippings as a punishment that I deserved.

About two, the party started breaking up. Most of the guests were high on liquor and marijuana and some of them were sprawled out unconscious or asleep in the living room. Little Bits gave me a man's overcoat to wear home. My own clothes were in rags.

"Here's two thousand," she whispered, "I pay you a thousand and you made a hit with a certain gentleman and he gave you a thousand for a tip, but don't tell the other girls. He wants to have another session with you sometime—can I expect you to come back?"

"Sure," I answered.

I was too scared to say no and in some ways, I wanted to. The air outside felt clean and cool and I sucked it deep into my lungs. It helped to drive away some of the haze. Part of me said that it had been a dream, but another part of me said it had been, real—too real.

I was sure glad to see Green street again. There had been moments at Little Bits' when I hadn't been sure that I would.

CHAPTER NINETEEN

WHEN I WOKE UP the next morning, I was sick, not physically sick but mentally sick. I couldn't keep my mind off the hours of shame that I had gone through the night before and it gave me the shakes. Rosie had some whiskey. I drank it and ordered another bottle from the drug store and I told them to hurry with it. For breakfast, I had whiskey and water.

A man banged on the front door, but I told Rosie not to answer it. I couldn't stand the sight of a man, let alone do anything with him. I was a mess; my hair and face a sight. He banged on my front door for about five minutes and I thought he was going to kick it in. He wanted me bad, but it was tough because I didn't want him or his money. Not right now, but I knew that in an hour or so, I would be kicking myself for not taking him on.

Finally, he went away.

They had hired a new guy to take Bill's place and he came around. He was strictly a punk. He was about twenty-five and had just done time for armed robbery with intent to kill. I think that's what they called it. He tried to act tough, real tough in front of us, and he had a cigarette dangling from the corner of his lips.

"There's a successful little juvenile deliquent if I ever saw one," Rosie commented.

She took my bottle away from me and tried to get me to drink some coffee but I wanted to get drunk. I wanted to get good and drunk and for a few moments forget that there was such a thing as sex. The few times that I have been drunk, I have imagined this to be a sexless world. It was a delightful place to be and I was feeling that way now.

"Why can't we be like insects or something?" I looked up at Rosie, "When I took biology or something, I saw a little bug under a microscope. Know what he did? He just divided himself in two. He didn't go to all the bother we do." I shook my finger at Rosie, "Did you ever stop to think how much trouble sex is? Rosie, it ain't worth the trouble."

I made a sweeping motion with my hand and knocked over my glass.

"Girl, are you packing a load," Rosie said.

She made me stand outside in the clear air for awhile, then fed me some coffee. I got the giggles for awhile, but I came out of them when I got sick. Rosie held my head while I threw up.

"Why didn't you let me stay drunk?" I cried.

"Cause you're a working girl," Rosie answered. "You've got to meet your public with a smile whether you feel like it or not."

She helped me to dress and make myself presentable for my customers. I didn't remember that I had a date with Tom until Lois showed up at noon. I didn't feel like facing him, but I knew I couldn't stay away from him. I was in the mood to talk to him and tell him about myself.

I was busy in my room with a date when I heard Tom's clear voice in the parlor. My entire body froze with fear.

"Are you Mrs. Wanda Lane?" I heard him ask Lois.

"No, Honey, Wanda is busy with a customer," Lois answered. "I'm Lois, would you want to go to bed with me instead?"

I sprang out of bed and remembered to put on my robe. I was fumbling with the snaps when I flung the door open.

"Tom!" I called.

I stopped; my voice caught in my throat. The way Tom stared at me made tears of shame spring into my eyes. Shame was a bitter taste in my throat and I tried to look at him, but the look on his face made my eyes sink to the floor.

"Tom, I—I can explain," I stammered.

"Here's your driver's license. I—I thought you might need it." He drew up his shoulders and let them fall, "I don't think there's anything to explain. You made a fool of me, I just hope you had a lot of fun doing it."

He turned and opened the door. I ran towards him, grabbed him and tried to hold him back. I was crying so hard that I could hardly talk or see. Tom jerked away and flung me against the door.

"There's nothing to explain, I've had it—yeah, I've really had it," he snarled. "The way you deceived me and led me on—thinking—you were a nice girl. Yeah, nice girl—Today—today, I was bragging to some guys about the swell girl I had—how I was going to marry her. When I told them your name, they started laughing."

"It—it doesn't matter," I sobbed. "I—I love you—"

"You—talking of love?" Tom sneered. "And saying it doesn't matter. It does matter—it matters a lot—Do you think that—"

He was too angry to talk anymore. He drew back his hand and slapped me as hard as he could. It sent me reeling against the door. I had seen the blow coming, but I didn't try to duck it. I wanted him to hit me. I wanted him to use his fists on me. I wanted him to hurt me worse than I had hurt him. He stepped off the porch and started to leave. I started after him, but Rosie grabbed me. She held me with both arms and I struggled to get loose.

"Tom!" I screamed.

"It's—stay here," Rosie said.

Tom was in his car and was gone. He didn't look back. Rosie let go of me and I ran to the gate and stared uselessly at the empty street. I didn't have the strength to go after him. My customer was staring at me. Lois took his arm and led him into Rosie's bedroom.

"Do—do you think he—he'll come back to me?" I looked at Rosie.

"I don't know. You can't tell about those kind of men. They're pretty funny," Rosie answered. "All you can do is wait and see."

She was saying no, but trying to let me down easy. I went back into my room and sat down on the bed. How low can a person get? I asked myself. I wanted to cry, but I had no tears to cry with. All I could do was think and remember. My darling Tom. I remembered something so beautiful that had turned out so cheap and ugly. There was a bottle of lysol on my stand and I put it to my lips. It burned my mouth and throat, but I forced myself to keep on drinking. When the burn hit my throat, I started screaming.

CHAPTER TWENTY

The doctor at the hospital told me that all I got out of the deal was a burned mouth. When I came to, I could still taste the awful stuff in my mouth and when they brought me my dinner, I couldn't eat it. The food tasted like it had been cooked in lysol. They let Rosie in to see me that afternoon.

"Did Tom ever come back?" I asked the first thing. Rosie shook her head.

"Lois called him up and tried to explain about your hustling," Rosie answered. "He just said 'I'm sorry' and hung up. Men are funny that way." She paused and looked at me, "How do you feel?"

"I'll be all right now, honest. I've got everything out of my system," I answered and tried to smile at her. "O.K., now tell me the news."

"Same old grind—it never changes," she answered, "Goren, that new fall guy, he's fallen for Micky—that little red-head at Grace's. Goren told Micky's pimp to hit the road and that Micky was his factory now."

"How'd Micky take it?"

"She doesn't care," Rosie shrugged her shoulders. "One pimp is as good as another."

They kept me in the hospital until the next morning before they released me. For some reason, I felt light-hearted and gay. While I was there, I hadn't even minded the nurses and internes peeking into my room and staring at me like I had three heads. I took a taxi home.

There was no doubt in my mind that Tom and I were through. It was all over and somehow, it seemed that it had happened years ago, not yesterday. Rosie was so glad to see me that she grabbed me and kissed me when I walked in on her. She told me that John's lawyer had been trying to get hold of me. I called him long distance and he told me the news. John had pleaded guilty and had thrown himself on the mercy of the court. He had drawn a five to ten year rap.

"Do you want me to start divorce proceedings?" he asked.

"No—no, I changed my mind," I answered and hung up.

I changed my clothes and got ready to face my customers the way I had always done. I felt no different than I had before. The laundry man came and we dickered over how many towels I would need the way we had always done and that was no different. Goren, the punk, came around to collect. He acted tough and snarled at us. I watched him from the window. He went into Grace's and stayed for about an hour.

When he came out, his hat was cocked to one side of his head and he walked with a bigger swagger than usual. A car pulled up beside him and three pimps got out. Goren stopped; his hands hanging slack at his sides. Two of them grabbed him from behind and held his arms while Micky's guy went to work with a pair of brass knuckles. He took his time, carefully placing each blow. Micky sat in her window and quietly watched them. They left Goren lying on the sidewalk; his face a bloody pulp. He lay there for an hour before an ambulance came and took him away.

On this street, you see no evil, hear no evil, and speak no evil.

Two days later, Thomas dropped by to see me. I was alone and I had waited until he had caught me alone. I locked the door and pulled down all the blinds. He sat down on the sofa, lit a cigarette, and kept looking at me as if he couldn't make up his mind about something.

"I heard you tried to take a fall," he said.

"I'm O.K. now—you don't have to worry about me," I answered. "I'll hold up my end of the bargain."

I meant it too. Suddenly, I was conscious of being up against the wall with Thomas running his finger up and down my bra strap. Soberly, I stared at the wall, wondering what the right thing to say and do was.

"Do you ever do it just for love?" he asked.

"Not any more," I managed to look at him. Something about him scared me, but I didn't know what or why.

"Why?"

"A girl doesn't get hurt that way," I shrugged my shoulders. But I looked up at him and gave him a smile that I knew would make him think I was lying. I saw the look in his eyes and I wasn't scared of him so much. He was just like all the other men who came to me. The only difference was that he was a cop and he owned part interest in the factory. Maybe that was why I was scared of him.

"I've often wondered when you were going to get around to me again," I said.

"Do you want me to?" His breath was loud and heavy.

"Yes, I've been wanting you to," I answered.

He drew me close, kissed me, then lifted me into his arms and carried me into my bedroom the way a man carries a bride over the threshold. I giggled like a school girl.

Thomas was married and had a family. When he was through with me, he would go back to his wife. I wanted it that way. It kept everything simple, no complications. I had learned my lesson. From now on, I was going to keep my loving on a cash basis and I wasn't going to get involved with any damn man.

I fooled Thomas the way that I had fooled the other men. I made him think that I really wanted him and that I enjoyed doing it with him. He wanted to think that and I knew how to make it easy for him to believe it. I didn't put my clothes on afterward. Even though he was through with me, he wanted to have me naked and feel my body with his hands. I put my arms around him, drew my body close to his so he could smell my perfume. We lay there, not moving, our heads on the same pillow.

"Honey, there used to be four of us, but with Bill gone, it leaves only three, right?" I asked. He nodded, "If we could only buy out Jergens, there would only be two of us—right?"

I made Thomas laugh. He pushed me from him and sat up, reaching for the cigarettes on the stand table. He was still chuckling when he lit one.

"Wanda, you are a whore and you really meant it when you said you kept romance on a cash basis," he said. "One way or another, you intend to get paid every time you put out, don't you? You took a trip with me and you had it figured out how you were going to collect for it."

"I didn't mean it that way, honest," I said.

I sat up and put my arms around his neck, but he took them down. My body and my perfume weren't having any effect on him now.

"Don't bother lying to me," Thomas said, but he wasn't angry, "I like you this way. I know where we stand and that I'll make dough off of you."

"I want to make a little of that money myself," I answered.

He gave me a surprised look. When he started to stand up, I grabbed him and pulled him back down.

"Wait! There's something I want to explain," I said. He sat down; looking at me. I wondered how I could explain.

"I—I know what you think of me—that I'm pretty heartless or something. But try and look at it from my side, will you? I won't be young and pretty very long and in a few years, the men won't have anything to do with me. I don't mind asking a man to go to bed with me, but I don't want to end up begging them the way some girls have to. Do you understand what I mean?"

Thomas was silent for a moment; puffing thoughtfully on his cigarette.

"I won't double cross Jergens, but I'll see that you get every break that I can," he said slowly. "See you around, Honey."

For some reason, the house seemed awful lonely and empty after he left. I turned up the radio as loud as I could. Thomas could add and divide as well as I could. Guys like Thomas and Jergens were guys that I had to carry on my back in order to stay in business. But Thomas was hungry for money and I knew he would figure it the way I did. Before long, Jergens would be one less that I would have to carry.

I wondered how Thomas would pull it and wished I knew the deal between them. But he'd give Jergens a raw deal and just thinking about that, trying to picture the look on Jergen's face, when it happened, made me feel good.

CHAPTER TWENTY-ONE

IN LEVITICUS, it reads that it is better for a man to cast his seed into the belly of a whore than onto the ground. Perhaps, even God recognizes the need for women like me, and perhaps, prostitutes won't be so damned in the next world. One of the things that has caused me to wonder is that a man is allowed to redeem himself, but a woman isn't. A drunk can quit drinking or a criminal can reform and the world will treat him like a hero. But a woman? She's told to get back to the whorehouses where she belongs. The only way a chippy can reform, is to move far away, change her name, dye her hair, and hope that none of her customers ever recognize her. If someone does, she might as well hang out the red lantern.

There is a poem, a verse that I dearly love. I have it written down on a scrap of paper and keep it in my dresser. Sometimes, I'll open the drawer, read it slowly, and go about my business with the little comfort it gives me.

Some there are who tell
Of one who threatens he will toss to hell
The luckless Pots he marr'd in making—Pish!
He's a good fellow and all will be well

I have read that no custom, tradition, or institution will survive unless it is useful or needed. Whether this is true of prostitution or not, I will leave to the men in ivy towers to debate. Whether

I am a necessity or an unneeded evil, I don't know, but I do know that many men have taken advantage of my availability. Somehow, I doubt if prostitution has changed very much since the days of Rahab.

Nor has the tons of material written about the evils of prostitution served to keep women out of the brothels. I think that just as many have been eager to become prostitutes now as there ever has been. There was hardly a week went by that some woman didn't ask me to take her on. They ranged all the way from teen-agers on up to women in their late forties. The stock excuse that they all gave was that they needed the money and I suppose it would take a doctor to find out their real reasons.

During the next few months, I spent long and hard hours following my profession. A brothel looks a lot different from the inside out than it does from the outside looking in. There is nothing glamorous, exciting, or romantic about prostitution. If it's anything, it's just a monotonous but lazy way of earning a living.

I don't hate the men who come to me, whether they are nice to me or if they try to abuse or shame me. I've learned not to expect or hope for too much from my customers. I try to show them a good time and give them their money's worth. If I got a "thank you" or a kind word, I'm satisfied.

I ran my house as a place of business. I had to in order to stay in business. Competition is pretty keen along Green street and when it came to a customer, it was every girl for herself. Each morning, I would drive around town in my convertible to advertise Miss Wanda Lane. I guess everyone in town got to know my face and my car and my name. I had reached the point where I felt no shame when women stared at me when I drove down the street or if men let out cat calls.

The only thing that caused a ripple along Green street was that they found the man who had run over Bill. It *had* been an accident.

I heard from John occasionally and I answered his letters. He said he was doing fine and asked me to visit him. I never did. I knew I would break down if I did. Occasionally, I saw Tom when I went up town, but he would always look the other way. I knew that it was over between us and I mailed back the ring he gave me. In my letter that I tried to write, I tried to explain things. But it was impossible. The words wouldn't come out on paper, so I mailed the ring back without a word.

I was the most popular and most notorious prostitute on Green street. My total earning were a third greater than any other chippy on the street, but I also hustled more hours than any of them did. I kept my sign on and my door open eighteen to twenty hours at a stretch. I would doze in the chair beside the window while Rosie watched the street for dates.

The small hours of the morning were the hardest. The street outside was vacant and silent. I would sit and wait, and often for no reason at all, would burst out crying. Once, I called home, but when my father heard who was calling, he hung up without saying a word. When they learned I had become a prostitute, that was it. They have told the people back home that I am dead. My mother can't forgive me and she won't even answer my letters. I just hope that God won't be too angry with me.

Yet, most of the time, I didn't mind being a prostitute, and like most of the women in this business, I felt that a woman who worked in a store or factory was a sucker. She could earn a lot more a lot easier, just by selling it. I helped several women place themselves in whorehouses.

Despite the fact that we are outcasts, prostitutes, especially the ones in houses of prostitution, have certain business ethics.

The first one is to always protect the identity of a customer. If she wanted to, a Madame could engage in blackmail and so could some of her prostitutes. But a man's name and reputation is safe in a brothel as far as the girls are concerned.

One of the hardest rules to learn is never to speak to a customer out in public. It gives a girl a jolt to have a guy come to her, joke and be real friendly with her, then to meet him out in public and see him turn his head because he's afraid she'll speak to him.

There are few prostitutes who will stoop to rolling a drunk or to steal money from a customer. In real life, it is the other way around. A prostitute is in constant danger of being knocked in the head by a thug pretending to be a customer. I keep my money hidden in the kitchen and carry only enough to make change in my room.

Once in broad daylight, while Rosie and I were gone, someone broke in and ransacked the house. They took about a hundred dollars and a diamond ring of mine. The police never found them.

But our greatest worry is pickpockets. You would be surprised at the number of men who have their minds on other things when they get into bed with me, and a prostitute soon learns that her bra or her stocking top is a very poor place to store her roll. I've found that the safest place to carry money is in my shoe. It's pretty hard for a customer to explain why he wants to take my shoe off when we're in bed. Still, I've had guys who tried it.

Early one morning, almost three months after Bill's death, Thomas called me and told me that I was to be at the Longbow Hunting Lodge at seven that night. But he wouldn't tell me why. It was the first time I had seen or heard from Thomas in several months. I gave Lois a call and she agreed to hustle for me.

The lake was about seven miles west of town and Longbow Hunting Lodge was set on a secluded part of the north beach. It was supposed to be an exclusive hunting club for millionaires and the like. To keep from being recognized, I drove Lois' car and I was stopped twice by men on the road up to the lodge. They searched the car and I had to prove to them who I was. I had never seen any of the men before.

When I got to the lodge, the yard was filled with cars. I was stopped again at the front door and had to wait until someone identified me. It was Grace. She took me inside.

Gathered in the bar were five big time politicians, several of the owners of the gambling joints and night clubs, and two Madames from Green street; Grace and a Madame named Doris. Chief of Police Smith was there, acting very nervous and laughing in a high pitched voice at every little joke. There were other men there whom I recognized as either being on the city council or holding some county political office. From the talk, I gathered that this wasn't the first meeting like this.

A man, now a judge, who was running for the state legislature or something, stood up and banged on the bar for order. The men sat down at the tables.

"Now folks, I'll be straight about it and right to the point," the judge said. "If the other boys get in, you can look for things to be shut up tighter than a drum. Now, you've read the speeches that Johnson (the opposition mayor) has been making and I don't have to tell you that he'll follow them up."

"What's it going to cost us?" a gambler spoke up. He didn't seem mad or anything. He had just asked a simple question, the same way he might have asked what time it was.

"It's going to cost plenty to beat them," the judge answered.

"How much is it going to cost us?" the gambler repeated. He threw his cigarette into the fireplace.

"About thirty thousand."

"O.K." He shrugged his shoulders and walked out. The other gamblers followed him.

"Now, how much can you ladies raise?" The judge turned towards us with a flimsy smile.

"We can't raise thirty grand," Grace answered.

"We were thinking about twenty."

I watched Grace bite her lip. The other Madame coughed.

"May I ask a question?" I asked. The judge looked at me with surprise and nodded.

"What's this all about? Why should we raise money for you?"

"It's like this; we keep you open and give you protection. If the other party gets in, they'll put you out of business. It's that simple," he answered, then looked at Grace. "Can you raise twenty thousand on Green street?"

Grace nodded.

That was it. They had got what they wanted from us and Grace told me later that the reason they had called us together like that was that they had been expecting a squawk from the gamblers. Otherwise, they would have come around and told us.

Grace, Doris, and I met in a roadhouse that night. We went over the list of Madames and based the tab on the number of girls they were keeping. It came out roughly five hundred for each girl and five hundred for each Madame. My share was a thousand dollars.

"How come I was called to that meeting?" I asked. "I'm just a chippy."

"Don't let them kid you," Doris answered. "You've got more pull than you think."

In a week's time, we raised the twenty grand and two weeks later, we got the word to raise another ten grand. They were taking almost every dime that we were making.

On election night, the party that was in took a beating. Johnson won by a landslide. I turned off the TV and went to bed. Two nights later, I got a call from Thomas to be at the Longbow. Grace and I went together. Every Madame on the street watched us leave and were waiting for us to come back. It was funny, but all this was above the heads of the girls. They hardly knew or seemed to care what was going on. They knew that the street might be closed, but it meant nothing to them except a move to another brothel.

"Here comes the whipping," Grace said with a wry smile when we went into the hunting lodge.

The same Madames and gamblers were there, but the others had changed. I recognized Johnson from his photos and then I almost fell in my tracks. Thomas was the new chief of police. Johnson didn't say anything. He just sat back and listened, but his campaign manager did the talking and he had plenty to say.

"Now, you folks gave and gave plenty to the other guys," he said and tried to make it sound like we had done something wrong. "We ought to close you down for it, but we won't. We'll let things stand like they are."

"What about the Sheriff?" one of the gamblers asked. "He's a renegade now."

It took me a moment to figure out what he meant. The Sheriff still had two years to serve on his term and he was about the only one of the old party still in office.

"He's your headache, we can't do a thing with him," Johnson laughed. "There's nothing to keep him from closing you down if he wants to and remember, he'll be up for re-election in two years."

"Then he's your problem as much as he is ours," I said. "Just think of the smear that he could give your side. But can he raid the houses that are inside Parkville?"

"There's nothing that can stop him," Johnson nodded. He rubbed his chin with his finger, "However, there is another point. I made some promises to the voters and I should like to keep them. I want things a little more quiet on Green street. For example, take down those horrible neon signs."

We went home, a little worried. We had been given a lease on life, but it sounded like a short one. The only difference between the old and the new party was that we now paid graft to new faces. But the amounts remained the same. Jergens called and wanted to sell his share of the business for five thousand dollars. I was afraid to buy him out.

Two days later, the Sheriff had himself a ball. He was a renegade and he was playing it to the hilt. Instead of waiting until his election came up, he was beating the incumbent party to any glory. The front page of the morning paper showed him lustily swinging an ax to a roulette wheel. The rumor that hit the street was that we were next on the list.

We did what the mayor asked us to do. The neon signs came down and the fronts of the houses were dark. We sat in unlighted windows and watched the street. We were still there, but if you drove down the street, you might suppose that we were gone. We took customers in through the back door and only at night.

When I read the morning paper, I decided to take a long chance. I called the Sheriff on the phone and asked him to meet me.

"What for?" he almost bit my head off.

"Maybe we can work out a deal," I said.

He hung up on me. I figured it was over, but about three in the morning, he knocked on my back door. I turned out the lights and we sat in the darkness.

"What kind of a deal did you want to make?" he asked.

"I can give you third interest in my joint, if you'll keep the street open."

"No dice."

"Why not, you've taken money from this street," I snapped.

"Yeah, I have—so did the boys who were in office, but those days are gone," he said. "Have you been reading anything in the papers besides the funnies?"

"Orphan Annie is sad enough for me."

"There's been a couple of preachers trying to get this street closed. They helped get the old guys out and the new guys in," the Sheriff explained. "Johnson doesn't want to keep the whorehouses anyway."

I stared in the darkness at his shadow and heard him chuckle.

"There's a vice mob that wants to move into Parkville. The town gets a reputation for being a nice town and the boys in power have been promised more graft than the way things are now," the Sheriff chuckled. "They can arrest any whore who doesn't hustle for the mob and make a good showing on them. They won't have whores on just one street, they'll be all over town—out in the residential district, the hotels, even in the taxies. It'll be ten times worse than having the whorehouses."

A match flared bright and orange in the darkness and I caught a glimpse of his eyes when he lit a cigarette. They were blue and steady.

"Even if Johnson wanted to keep the whorehouses, the preachers wouldn't let him," he continued. "So when they crack this street, they'll bust it wide open and they'll show who owned what. That'll go for your fanny too."

I sat there in the darkness and drummed my fingers against the table.

"There's been a Grand Jury formed and they are going to start asking questions," he said.

"So to protect the boys, you've got to raid us. Is that it?"

"I'm afraid it is."

"How much time have we got?"

"Until two tomorrow morning," he answered. "Tell the Madames to get some of their girls out of town," he gave a long pause. "What about you?"

"I'm pretty big, ain't I?" I said slowly. "I guess it would look funny if I wasn't here."

"I'm afraid it would."

"I'll leave the front door unlocked—don't bust it down."

That day, I spread the word to the other Madames. They didn't act too surprised and they started telling some of their girls to get out of town. I rented a hotel room and moved most of my clothes and the things I valued most to it. I stored my jewelry in the hotel safe. I burned any records that I could find.

Rosie stayed with me until almost nine that night and then I made her pack up and leave. We kissed each other good-by and both of us were crying when the taxi came for her. I settled down to wait.

The raid was quiet and business-like. None of the girls knew that it was coming off and several were caught in bed. When two deputies led me out of the house, a news photographer took my picture. I threw my shoe at him. We spent two hours in police court and were released on five hundred dollars bail.

The next day, we pleaded guilty either to being an inmate of a house of prostitution or a keeper of a house of prostitution. Our fines were five hundred dollars apiece. The judge ordered the brothels to be padlocked for a year and a day. It meant that Green street was no more. It would probably never return. I was given twenty-four hours to get out of town.

I had saved no money. The fines, the rake-offs, and the contributions to the campaign elections had bled me white. I had to let my car go back and I cried when they took my beautiful white convertible away and put it on the sales lot. I had no choice but to sell my furniture to a dealer. All that I had to show for my efforts was two steamer trunks of clothes and about two hundred and fifty dollars. I probably could have done better working at the dime store.

I called Little Bits, the Madame who ran the brothel in Marshal, and told her my story. She said she would be glad to keep me. Whether I went to her sex parties or not depended on me, but I knew that I would. I wanted my convertible back.

Just for luck, I called Tom Sterling. When I told him my name, he hung up. When I went to the bus depot, a man handed me a box of candy. Inside, I found a note that said, "Thanks" and five hundred dollars. I was sure that Thomas sent it.

Little Bits ran the only whorehouse in town and it was upstairs over a vacant drug store on a dark side street. The men came in through the drug store and up the rear inside stairs. The bedrooms were in a row down a narrow dimly lit corridor and we waited in our bedrooms for the men. When a man came into my room, Little Bits would punch a hole in a card that I carried. I got two bucks for every hole she punched. My first day and night there, I took on sixty men.

I was there two days when a pimp came into my room. I was sitting on my bed, fixing my face.

"Little Bits says you ain't got no man," he said.

"No, I'm on my own."

"Now, that's no way for a gal to be," he said. "A gal like you needs someone to take care of her. I'll be your man." It was as simple as that. I didn't have anyone to stand up for me and even if I had, I wouldn't have asked him to. For some reason, I just didn't care anymore. Sam, my new pimp, had another girl hustling for Little Bits. He waited in his car and at closing time, Little Bits would throw our cards down the stairs to him, so we wouldn't try to hold any money back from him.

One night, I had pulled back the blind to get some air and I saw Tony drive up. The pimp who had tried to move in on me in Parkville. I watched him and Sam talk for a moment, then Tony took a punch at Sam. I watched their shadows move back and forth as they fought. They were fighting over me, but who won didn't seem important.

It was Tony who came up the stairs. He came to my room and paused at the threshold. His lips were bleeding, his shirt torn, and his shoulder had been rubbed raw against the concrete.

"You're my girl now," he stated in a flat voice. I guess he expected me to argue, but I didn't.

"I know," I said. "Come here and let me fix your face—you're a mess."

He sat down on the bed and I washed the blood off his face. A customer knocked on my door and I called out, "Busy," without turning my head.

"Tony, be good to me, will you?" I whispered.

"I will, Baby, I will," he promised.

I looked into his face. He wasn't much of a man, but a woman like me couldn't expect very much in a man. Tony was about all that a whore like me could expect or hope for. I looked at him and smiled.

"I'll earn you plenty," I promised.

He went on out, leaving my door open. My room seemed cold and empty. A man came down the hallway, I wiped away a tear and smiled at him. I hoped God wouldn't be too angry with me.

THE END

www.ingramcontent.com/pod-product-compliance
Lightning Source LLC
Chambersburg PA
CBHW022200240626
47153CB00007B/2757